BLOOD ON CANVAS

A C.T. FERGUSON CRIME NOVELLA

THE C.T. FERGUSON CRIME NOVELLAS
BOOK 4

TOM FOWLER

Cover design by 100 Covers

Editing by Chase Nottingham

CHAPTER 1

I WAS ABOUT TO TAKE MY FIRST BITE OF STREET CORN when I got the question I'd hoped not to hear. "Mister Ferguson, what do you think of the painting?"

I sat in the Hacienda Mexican Restaurant. Its co-owner, Juan Manuel Espinoza, awaited my answer. My potential client referred to an image hanging on the brick wall near our table. It was maybe eighteen inches by two feet and surrounded by a tacky wooden frame I would have been embarrassed to use as kindling.

This wasn't the worst part of it, however. The painting depicted the face of Jesus on a black background. I'd never been adept at drawing, and I felt pretty confident I could've done better. The proportions of the head were odd, with the chin too large and the forehead small by comparison. Jesus' hair appeared stringy, his beard too long, and the dimensions of the crown of thorns on his head could have formed a hat. After a few seconds of consideration, I managed to say, "Um."

A polished speaker, I am.

The painting was hideous. However, Espinoza proudly pointed it out to me when we sat down. I didn't want to tell him what I thought of the art. It struck me as akin to telling a mother her baby was ugly. Even if the tyke made strangers want to cover their eyes, one didn't go around pointing it out.

Thankfully, he let me off the hook. "It is ugly. I know."

It enjoyed plenty of company. The restaurant displayed quite a few works of art, and many of them strained the term's definition. Hacienda earned a good reputation for their food over the years. If the fare had been mediocre, more people might have noticed what hung on the walls. The few other people in the dining area took notice of nothing but their meals and each other. "I didn't want to come out and tell you," I said.

"I understand." He spread his hands. "As I told you, it's a copy. The original was stolen recently."

"I don't mean to sound indelicate, but why would someone steal an ugly painting?"

"This is why I want to hire you," Juan Manuel said. His voice carried only a mild accent. While he talked, a waiter came out with my entree—three assorted tacos, plus rice and refried beans. When the server walked away, Juan Manuel gestured at my glass of iced tea. "You don't want a margarita?"

"I find alcohol dulls my appreciation of art," I said. I finally ate a few bites of my street corn, and while it had grown lukewarm during the conversation, it still tasted terrific.

The owner smiled. "I think you would need many margaritas to find it pretty."

I examined the tacos on my plate. Judging by the thin cut of meat and fragrant spices, I pegged the first as carne asada. The middle was some sort of chicken, and the remaining one a variety of fish. Being a proud American carnivore, I started with the beef. It possessed just the right amount of heat. I devoured the taco before I knew it. "Why do you want to find the original?" I asked after wiping my mouth. "You've admitted it's ugly. I can't imagine it's very valuable."

"It has been in my family for three generations," Juan Manuel said. "My grandfather was great friends with the artist. Our families remain close to this day."

"Sentimental value, then." He nodded. Juan Manuel's graying hair and crow's feet put him around sixty. "Your grandfather would have acquired the painting about a hundred years ago, then?"

"*Más o menos*," he said. "Are you familiar with the Escobar Rebellion?"

I shook my head. "Not really."

"It happened in Mexico. Nineteen twenty-nine."

"It probably gets drowned out by the other big event of the same year."

Juan Manuel showed me a small smile. "They don't teach you much Mexican history in schools here."

"I know Mexico's independence day is in September, not the fifth of May," I said. "Puts me one up on about ninety percent of my countrymen."

He laughed and clapped his hands. "Very well. I can forgive you not knowing about the Escobar Rebellion. It was not a long conflict. My grandfather served in the national army along with his friend Gerardo Garza. Toward the end, some of the battles were brutal. *Señor* Garza participated willingly, according to my grandfather. In the year after, he came to regret it. He rediscovered religion and took up painting." He paused. "Are you a religious man, Mister Ferguson?"

"Call me C.T.," I said. "And no . . . not particularly."

Juan Manuel shrugged. "I don't think my grandfather was, either. He remained friends with *Señor* Garza for many years. As I told you, our families are still close. You can always spot a Garza because he signs each painting with his initials."

I scanned the copy on the wall. Sure enough, in the lower left corner, I noticed a small *GG* in white letters to stand out against the black background. "Is this the only one you have?"

"No," Juan Manuel said. "We keep some in the basement. The original of this one was always on display. Otherwise, my son decides what goes on the walls."

"He's your partner in the restaurant?" I returned to my neglected meal, taking a large bite of the chicken taco.

"He is." Juan Manuel beamed. "Miguel was the first of our family to finish college."

"Congratulations," I said around a mouthful of food.

"*Gracias*. Miguel and I dislike showing this copy. Do you think you can help me find the original?"

I'd never worked an art theft case before, so I had no insights into it. I also couldn't fathom why somebody would steal an ugly painting whose value was largely sentimental. Maybe the thief knew, which would make it a personal crime. "I can," I said. "I'll probably need some information from you along the way. If the painting isn't worth much, I have to think someone stole it to hurt you personally."

My host grimaced at my comment. "What you say is possible. I will help you any way I can."

"All right. I'll start as soon as I finish my dinner."

"You don't work for money?"

"No," I said, "but I might need a few hundred more of these tacos."

"It can be arranged," Juan Manuel said with a smile.

I DROVE BACK to my house in the Federal Hill area of Baltimore. Like many old parts of the city, homes topped a century in age. I owned an end-unit rowhouse which was tall and fairly deep but not especially wide. I swung my Audi S4 into the alley which runs parallel to my street and pulled onto the parking pad behind my house. A familiar red rocketlike Mercedes coupe occupied the other half.

Sure enough, my girlfriend Gloria Reading arrived while I was gone. She greeted me with a kiss after I opened the back door and walked into the kitchen. "What's for dinner?"

"I ate three really good tacos."

"You brought some for me, right?" I made a show of looking at everything in the room except Gloria. This was difficult, as I could never tire of gazing at her. She angled her head to the side and pointed at the plastic bag tucked behind my leg. "You did!"

I held the bag out. "Enjoy. They're probably still hot."

A couple minutes later, we sat at the table in my kitchen. Calling it a breakfast nook overstated the available space. Whoever owned the house before me remodeled it to include a first-floor office and a small addition at the rear. The results were a cramped kitchen and negligible dining room. Considering Gloria and I ate most of our meals on the couch or in restaurants, the tradeoff was worth it.

I kept it simple and got Gloria a trio of carne asada tacos plus a bowl of rice. Her proper upbringing compelled her to set a full place for herself at the table. "If you eat those with a knife and fork," I said, "I'm never bringing you tacos again."

Gloria looked between her meal and me. She smiled, picked up one folded tortilla, and took a massive bite. It was enough to make me do a double take. In addition to cutting her food like a well-mannered lady, Gloria always took small bites. What I could devour in four chomps took her ten. These tacos proved the exception. After she scarfed down the first one, she said, "Weren't you going to a Mexican restaurant to talk about a case?"

I nodded. "Apparently, I investigate missing paintings now."

"What do you know about art?"

"Not much," I said. "I skipped the class in college whenever I could."

Gloria chuckled around a bite of dinner. Once she

finished chewing and wiped her mouth, she said, "Me, too."

"And here I thought you enjoyed the 'arts' portion of your snooty liberal arts education." Gloria graduated from Brown, probably because her parents wanted to be able to boast about it at dinner parties. I eschewed the Ivy League for local Loyola College, and I've wondered if my mother missed the bragging point at rotary club meetings.

"Paintings and PowerPoint don't mix," Gloria said.

I let her finish the rest of her meal without going into details. Once she'd cleared the table and we adjourned to the living room, Gloria wanted to know all about the case. Early in our relationship when it was based on fun and convenience, she didn't take an interest in my work. Over time, she grew more curious about it, we made things official on the personal front, and Gloria began using her considerable brains and moneyed connections to work as a fundraiser. "Is it a famous painting?" she asked.

"What's the opposite of famous?" I said, leaning my head back on the comfortable couch.

Gloria snuggled up to me and put her head on my shoulder. "Who steals something obscure?"

"There's more." I called up a picture Espinoza sent me, showing the artwork in all its limited glory. She frowned and wrinkled her nose.

"It's hideous."

"Even the owner thinks so."

"Why does he want it back?"

"Sentimental value," I said. "His grandfather was good friends with the artist, and a bunch of these things are still in the family."

Gloria grabbed my hand and peered at the image on my phone. "Is it painted on velvet?"

"I don't think so, but it does look a little like it."

"You've worked some strange cases before," Gloria said, "but this one might be the weirdest. I can't imagine someone stealing that thing, and then I don't know why anyone would want it back."

"I had the same thoughts," I said. "It made me curious, so I told the restaurant owner I'd look into it."

Gloria shifted her head and kissed my neck. I wrapped my hand in her chestnut hair. "When were you planning on starting?" she said in a breathy whisper.

"I can't imagine the thing is in high demand. Tomorrow should be fine."

Gloria swung one leg over me and settled onto my lap. "I like the way you think."

THE NEXT MORNING, I woke up just before nine. Since turning thirty about seven months ago, I lost my ability to sleep in. On the whole, getting older beat the alternative, so I tried to reframe the early hour as getting a start on my morning constitutional. I left a sleeping Gloria in bed, changed into running attire, and hit the mean streets of Federal Hill.

Most mornings, I did my laps around the eponymous park, and today was no exception. The streets were quieter here. They got busier on the weekends when restaurants and bars pulled in good crowds. During the week, however, the hustle and bustle of Baltimore lay several minutes away on the other side of the harbor. To change up the routine some days, I went across Key Highway and ran around Harborplace. In the summer, though, the tourist count went way up, and I preferred not dodging a lot of people.

About thirty minutes later, I returned home and showered. Gloria remained in the exact same pose she was in when I left some forty minutes prior. I never knew how she slept through the water running nearby, but she always did. She'd be awake soon enough. I walked downstairs, put a pot of coffee on, and surveyed the food situation in my kitchen. A few minutes later, I cooked pancakes and turkey bacon in separate skillets. The combined aromas wafting up roused Gloria, as they always did. Her feet hit the hardwood, and she came down while I plated everything.

"Morning," she said, planting a minty kiss on me and fixing herself a mug of coffee. I watched her with interest. In the summer, Gloria's sleepwear grew smaller. She wore a scandalous tank top and a tiny pair of shorts which would've been considered indecent at the Playboy Mansion. My gaping drew her attention, and she smiled. "Easy, tiger. We're both hungry."

I couldn't speak for Gloria, but I certainly was. After wolfing three large pancakes and four slices of bacon, I felt ready to take on the day. As usual, Gloria finished eating after I did. I poured some coffee in a travel mug, kissed my barely-dressed girlfriend goodbye, and left while my resolve still held.

For about two years, I've kept an office in the Care-First Building in Canton Square. Shortly after I moved in, they took over from the previous owners. At this point, I was one of the very few tenants without a connection to medicine. I expected them to give me the boot at any time. Until then, I liked the separation from my personal life. Working from my house didn't allow for it, and one more look at Gloria would've ruined me for the rest of the morning.

Not knowing much about art and those who would steal it, I began with Google. I spent close to a half-hour reading about the thefts of paintings over the years, their recovery, and the investigators who figured it all out. If a bunch of faceless feds could sort these things out, I liked my odds. Next, I dug into Gerardo Garza and his many works. Like Juan Manuel told me, he painted endless pictures of Jesus. There were slight variations between them, but one thing remained true: all of them were ugly.

Why someone would go to the trouble of stealing a hideous piece of art remained puzzling to me. Garza wasn't famous. This wasn't a million-dollar Picasso someone swiped in the night. Using what Juan Manuel told me, I looked into the history and provenance of many Garza works. All origination in Mexico in the years following the Escobar Rebellion. The first changed hands in 1933. The 'forties and early 'fifties saw the most activity.

Following Garza's death in 1960, interest in his body of work spiked briefly before returning to ho-hum status. Much of his catalog ended up with the Espinoza family. Miguel Ángel, Juan Manuel's grandfather and the inspiration for his son's name, kept detailed records of what he maintained in his inventory. I found a scan of a Mexican newspaper article from 1963. Despite a bit of rust on my Spanish, I made it through the piece.

Jesús Sobre Terciopelo No. 35, which earned the name from its velvety appearance despite being painted on canvas, first appeared in the family's records in 1960. Sixty years later, someone stole it from a restaurant in Baltimore. It remained hideous throughout its history, and none of Garza's paintings held any real value on the open market.

Something beyond art theft was going on here, and I'd jumped headlong into it.

CHAPTER 2

I DROVE HOME FROM MY OFFICE WHEN A CALL CAME in. "Mister Ferguson, I have some news," Juan Manuel said.

"You decided a handsome detective shouldn't be looking for an ugly painting?"

"No," he said after a moment's hesitation. "It is something you might find useful. Could you come by the restaurant?"

"Can I take a few more tacos home?" When Juan Manuel answered in the affirmative, I told him I was en route. Ten minutes later, I left my car in the parking lot and walked inside. Juan Manuel waved me to the same table we shared earlier.

"Thanks for coming." He held his hand out toward the same chair I sat in before. "You know my family is not the sole owner of *Señor* Garza's works."

I nodded. "I looked into the provenance of as many of his paintings as I could find. You have the majority. The rest tend to be pretty sketchy."

"*Sí*. They are scattered. You may not think so to look at them, but the paintings were in demand for a while."

"Why am I here, Juan Manuel?"

"There is another Mexican *restaurante* a few miles from here . . . La Tolteca. They have another Garza on their walls." He paused and frowned. "They did, at least."

"Theirs got stolen, too?" A waiter approached, and I waved him off. The to-go order would cover Gloria and me for lunch tomorrow.

"I just heard about it. They don't display theirs as prominently as we do." His tone indicated this was a point of pride. I let it go. "They're not sure when it happened."

"Did they report it to the police?"

Juan Manuel shook his head. "Neither did I. The value in money isn't there. The police aren't going to spend a lot of time on it."

"Does *Señor* Garza have any living relatives?" I asked.

"A few . . . none around here, though. One descendant lives in Florida. The rest are still in Mexico." He paused. "Do you want to talk to Ricardo? He's the owner there. I could tell him you're coming."

"I don't think it'll help," I said. "They just noticed the painting is gone and don't know when it actually disappeared. Not a conversation I want to have."

Juan Manuel leaned closer and whispered. "What do you think is happening, Mister Ferguson?"

"C.T. And I'm not sure yet. I don't exactly have a long history of art theft cases to compare this to." I considered calling Agent Hess with the local FBI field office. Considering how useless I found him the last time I tried to involve him, however, I immediately thought better of it. If I were desperate for a lifeline later, I'd make the call.

"Good luck, then," Juan Manuel said.

A waitress set a stuffed paper bag onto the table in front of me. The smell of carne asada nearly compelled me to rip it open and devour a taco. "I'll need it," I said, "but these will help in the meantime."

* * *

The following morning, I met my cousin Rich at his precinct. He's a homicide sergeant in the Baltimore Police Department. When I first began my PI work, he served as a uniformed sergeant. Rich has always seen his ascension to the plainclothes ranks corresponding with my investigative endeavors as a mere coincidence. He's never been receptive to my argument of correlation equaling causation in this case.

I dropped a cup of hot coffee on his desk, and he picked it up with an appreciative nod. "What's going on?" At thirty-seven, Rich was six and a half years older than me, and I rarely missed a chance to point out how much he looked it. He kept his dark hair short like the army taught him, and today being a Tuesday, he wore his usual suit for this day of the week.

"Does the BPD investigate art theft at all?" I plopped into one of his uncomfortable guest chairs and remembered why I preferred standing when chatting with my cousin.

"Sure. It's right after murders, shootings, and gang violence on the priority list." He kept a straight face and sipped some coffee.

I partook of my delicious vanilla latte to avoid snapping off my usual sarcastic response. "Great. Let me know who I should talk to about it, then."

"You're really looking into art theft?"

"I was promised a lot of free tacos. It may have tipped the scales."

Rich grinned. "You know, if you want some help on this one, I work for food."

"I'm all right so far," I said. Sharing the tacos with Gloria proved difficult enough. I hoped she didn't raid the bag and eat them all while I was gone.

"Anyone dead in this case yet?" Rich asked.

"Looking at enough of these hideous paintings might do it."

"My partner and I have enough on our plate already." He paused and added, "Not a taco pun."

"Where is King, anyway?" Rich's partner, Detective Paul King, could be his mirror universe counterpart. He even sported the goatee. While Rich reserved a suit for each day of the week, King wore whatever he pulled from the closet in the morning. His mop of sandy blond hair stood in stark contrast to Rich's precision buzz cut. Despite looking like a rock singer who did one too many lines of coke, King was a capable detective, and he and Rich enjoyed a solid working relationship.

"Talking to O'Malley." Rich's face darkened at the mention of his lieutenant's name. I shared his low opinion of the man. In return, O'Malley didn't like me much, either, which I took as a sign I did things right. I followed his eyes and saw the nearby office door closed.

I lowered my voice. "Does anyone like him?"

Rich shook his head. "Someone upstairs must."

I stood. "I'll let you know if this turns into something else. You haven't earned a commendation for my work in at least a month."

Rich rolled his eyes. "You talk to the FBI?"

I scoffed. "Your buddy Hess is about as useful as a piece of glass in my shoe."

"You're being a little hard on him," Rich said.

While I took another preemptive drink of my latte, I recalled Hess' worthlessness in an important case last year. "Agree to disagree." Before Rich could attempt to defend his FBI buddy again, I left.

* * *

I DROVE from the precinct to my office. Two thefts of ugly paintings happened in a short amount of time. My job taught me years ago not to believe in coincidences. The odds of two different people stealing a pair of similar-looking pieces of art in a short timeframe were astronomical. The same person must have been on the hook for both, and I possessed no insights as to his or her agenda.

He would have told me, but I called to confirm the fact, anyway. Juan Manuel didn't have any security cameras and only deployed the most crude of alarms. It didn't go off when the thief stole the Garza. He suggested I call La Tolteca, so I did. Ricardo joined the line after I languished on hold for a few minutes while the restaurant couldn't have been busy. "You talked to Juan Manuel?"

"I did," I said. "He told me the same thing happened to you. It's likely the same person is responsible for both."

"Is there anything I can do?"

"Tell me you have a good security system."

"We are in luck," Ricardo said. "I upgraded a couple months ago."

I pumped my fist. Even though it was early, this struck me as a case where even little victories would count. "Excellent. Can you send me the footage?" I provided my email address.

"I will." Ricardo paused, and his deep breath filled the line. "Part of my new system is a standard alarm. It goes off if someone opens any of the doors or breaks a window."

When he lapsed into silence, I picked up the conversational slack. "Let me guess . . . the alarm didn't go off."

"You're right," he said.

"How many people know the code to disarm it?" I asked.

"I'm not sure."

I pinched the bridge of my nose and closed my eyes. Security systems, like anything else, can contain vulnerabilities. The biggest one was always the people who operated them. "It's something you really need to know and control. If everyone can disarm the blasted thing, it's almost pointless to have it."

"What should I do?" Ricardo asked.

"Change the code. Give the new sequence to as few

people as possible. Only those opening or closing the restaurant without you there. Every ninety days or so, do it again. In the near term, send me a list of anyone you can think of having access to the footage."

"All right." We hung up, and I shook my head. One owner barely had a system at all. The other's setup was outstanding but compromised by giving the code out to everyone. If only a small group possessed the right combination of digits, figuring out who broke in—or who helped the actual thief—would be easy. With a larger population sample, most employees at La Tolteca would be suspects.

About a half-hour later, the video and a text file with employee names hit my inbox. Besides Ricardo, fourteen people made the list, and the body of his email indicated he may have forgotten some. If he handed me the names on paper, I would have crumpled it up and thrown it at him. Instead, I could only seethe as I queued the footage.

Ricardo provided most of the night's surveillance, which included a lot of dead time. The restaurant closed at ten, the kitchen staffers wrapped up their work around eleven, and everyone was gone before midnight. They ran an efficient operation at La Tolteca. Too bad it didn't extend to basic security practices. Nineteen seconds after 2:04 AM, the back door opened slowly. A masked figure entered. Comparing the body to the doorframe, whoever walked in stood a little over six feet tall and weighed about two hundred pounds. Definitely a man. With the full-face mask, hood, long sleeves, gloves, and pants, I couldn't determine the crook's race, hair color, or eye color.

The mystery man glanced around for a few seconds. I

turned the volume down as the shrill alarm blasted through the kitchen. The burglar walked to the keypad, pushed a few buttons, and everything fell silent again. He got the code on the first try. Definitely an inside job. Either this man was an employee, or one of Ricardo's way-too-many trusted employees fed him the information.

The crook then jogged out of frame. Another camera picked him up moving through the restaurant, but he disappeared for long stretches of time. I wondered if this was due to poor camera placement or more insider knowledge. Probably a little of both. A few minutes after sneaking in the back door, the thief returned to the kitchen camera carrying something under his arm. It had to be the missing painting. He reset the alarm, opened the door, and left.

I fast-forwarded through the footage. Nothing happened the rest of the night, and the images ended at five o'clock. Ricardo's video didn't include any exterior cameras. I would have installed them. Of course, I would have done many things differently if this were my restaurant and my expensive defense system. Instead, I needed to sift through the pieces of what Ricardo provided.

Adding a few of my own of course would help. It only took a minute to access nearby surveillance video. Baltimore installed the system in my youth and added to it over time. Its security remained trapped in a bygone era, and only a rare stroke of good luck for the city saved it from frequent compromises. I found two cameras stationed near La Tolteca.

The mystery burglar appeared on both. I slowed the

play speed down to try and get a better look at him. While the city upgraded the technology a few times, resolution was not first among its virtues. I zoomed in as much as I could without losing too much detail. As far as I could tell, the thief wore his full outfit to and fro. I never got a look at his face or any piece of exposed skin. Whoever this was prepared himself for the possibility he'd be filmed throughout.

For a likely inside job at a Baltimore restaurant, it certainly possessed an air of professionalism.

CHAPTER 3

THE FOLLOWING MORNING, I AWOKE BEFORE GLORIA. This is part of our routine now. Her shapely right leg protruded from the sheet and blanket, testing my resolve as I changed into running clothes. I left her asleep as I hit the mean streets of Federal Hill for my morning constitutional. I live close to the neighborhood's eponymous park, and it's a frequent part of my runs. The view of the harbor and downtown on the Key Highway side is hard to beat.

About four miles later, I walked back toward my house. Two car doors opened, and a pair of men climbed out of the sedan. They were both Hispanic, stood at least as tall as me, and outweighed me by at least fifty pounds each. Before I began working as a private investigator, I never felt small at six-two and one-ninety. Now, it happened a few times a month.

They both stood in the sidewalk, and their combined size made them proficient at blocking it. I walked closer. Their eyes narrowed as they scrutinized me, focusing on my midsection in an inevitable weapons check. One of these weeks, I needed to wear a small gun when I went out for my morning exercise.

I stopped a few feet from them. The one on the left was a little taller than his partner, and a neck tattoo peeked out above the collar of his shirt. The other goon carried more weight on his frame, and his physique suggested he drank beer and did bicep curls in equal amounts. In Spanish, the taller one said, "I think we can take him." I stayed quiet. "Back off your case." Again, I offered no reply.

"I don't think he gets it," the man on the right said.

"Let me stop you there, guys," I said. "I speak Spanish pretty well, so if you're trying to intimidate me by thinking I can't understand you, it's not going to work." They glanced at each other and frowned. "I don't know French or German, though. If you do, you can talk to one another, and I'll do my best to stand here and look scared." This time, they could muster nothing for a retort. "How about Klingon?" Silence. "Or we can drop all this, you can threaten me in English, and I'll tell you to go to hell."

"Stop working your case," Neck Tattoo said. He clenched his meaty fists. It didn't add much to his intimidation value.

"Sure. Return the ugly paintings you stole, get out of my city, and we'll call it a draw."

"I was right," the fatter goon said. "You don't get it."

The inked fellow's weight shifted to the balls of his feet. He represented the greater threat. As his arm moved back, I gave him a quick kick in the family jewels to stun him, and then followed it with a boot to the face to put him down. I traded power for speed, so I didn't expect him to be out of the fight for long, but it allowed me to focus on the fatter one.

He lunged at me, and I stepped to the right. I spared a glance at the prone goon, who flexed his jaw and shook off the cobwebs. He wouldn't stay down much longer. When the shorter one threw another punch, I blocked it, hit him hard in the gut, and dropped him to the sidewalk with an elbow to the face. The other enforcer got back to his feet and glared daggers at me. "On second thought," I said, "I don't think French or German would've worked, either."

"*Puta*," he spat as he fired off some quick jabs. I let him advance, moving backward to be closer to the corner house behind us. When Neck Tattoo threw a haymaker, I grabbed his arm and whipped him into the nearby wall. His face bounced off it, so I took hold of his hair at the back of his head and rammed it into the brick a couple times. The lights went off, and I let him fall near his fellow goon.

Our scuffle attracted a couple onlookers across the street. To get out in front of things, I called the police.

* * *

A FEW MINUTES LATER, Officers Jennings and Brennan questioned me. They turned up often when I summoned the men in blue. Both were veteran cops a little older than me. We settled into our usual routine: they asked what I knew, I evaded, they grumbled, I evaded some more. "You're sure you don't know who these two are?" Jennings asked in a final attempt to pry some nugget of information out of me.

"I didn't check their IDs." I shrugged. "By now, I'm sure someone has." Four other cops and two paramedics milled about the scene. Both enforcers were conscious and receiving supervised medical attention. Neither looked happy about their current situation.

"You're not working a case?" Brennan said.

"Sure . . . a missing painting or two. I hate to typecast based on goonish appearances, but I don't think either of these two would make it as art critics."

"You know the drill," Jennings said. "If you think of anything . . ."

"I'll call you." I took his card when he offered it. One more for the collection. After finishing with the police, I walked the remaining block to my house. Gloria stirred when I got in the shower, and she was already downstairs when I emerged freshly dressed a short while later. Coffee brewed, and I took a moment to admire the aroma filling the kitchen.

"Longer run than usual?" Gloria said as she stood next to me at the counter and planted a minty kiss on my lips.

"I got some extra cardio today." I told her about the pair of goons trying to discourage me. "As usual, I take this to mean I'm on the right track."

"Be careful."

"Always," I said. I poured coffee for each of us, whipped up a quick breakfast of English muffins and sausage, and then bade Gloria farewell for the office.

After settling in and downing some more java, I called Paul King. "What do you know about art?"

"As little as possible," he said. "What do you have going on?"

"Two missing paintings—both ugly and both of Jesus—from Mexican restaurants. This morning, a couple of Hispanic tough guys tried to get me to drop the case."

"What happened?"

"Turns out they weren't so tough," I said. "You ever run across anything like this?" Before working as Rich's partner in homicide, King enjoyed a varied career in the BPD, including stints in both vice and narcotics.

"Not specifically," he said. "Can you describe the gentlemen you encountered this morning?" I gave him as many details as I could remember. "Probably drugs."

"Why?"

"Latino gangs are all over the place," King said. "They generate money in the ways you might expect. For years, they've basically avoided Baltimore. Your friend Tony didn't like anyone coming in and trying to sell powder to the fine people of this city." I declined to point out the frost which accumulated on my relationship with Tony Rizzo over the last several months. "Even mob bosses get old, though. Word is he's not running as tight a ship as he used to. It means a bunch of enterprising guys from somewhere south of the border can try and set up shop."

"I don't want to involve Tony if I don't need to," I said.

"Your call. He might be able to solve your problem with a few bullets."

"I'd prefer to handle it on my own."

"Anything else? The city ain't gonna keep itself safe."

"You'll never lack for job security," I said and broke the connection.

Drugs. Great.

CHAPTER 4

A LITTLE LATER IN THE DAY, I DROVE TO THE Esperanza Center. It sits on Broadway just north of Eastern Avenue. While most of Fells Point is known for eateries, taverns, and shops, the Esperanza Center provides important services for recent immigrants to the United States. It's a bit out of place in the neighborhood. When I first returned from Hong Kong about three years ago, I volunteered for a couple weeks before beginning my PI career.

The director I worked with then moved on in the interim. Her replacement, a woman with the title of Program Manager, was stuck in a meeting. Instead, I sat down with Father David Abbott, a Catholic priest who also worked as a case manager. We met in a small, sparse office. The reverend's bookshelves were filled with tomes on immigration, spirituality, and social work. I almost fell asleep reading the spines. A crucifix hung on the wall behind his desk. "What can I do for you, Mister Ferguson?"

Father Abbott looked to be in his mid-thirties. He was a white man with brown hair and green eyes. This made him an unusual fit for a facility which employed mostly Hispanic workers. "I've picked up an interesting case." I showed him my badge and ID.

"Interesting how?"

"Are you familiar with Hacienda?"

He nodded. "Good food. Juan Manuel and his family donate to the center every year."

"Then, you've probably also seen the . . . paintings of Jesus on the walls," I said.

"I have." The priest's eyes narrowed. "Where is this going?"

"One of those paintings disappeared. Stolen. The same thing happened from another restaurant."

"I can assure you we don't have them," Father Abbott said with a chuckle.

"I'm sure you don't. The Catholic Church can afford much better art. Where I'm struggling is why would someone steal a couple of ugly wall hangings?"

The reverend showed a toothy grin. "They are pretty hideous, aren't they? Don't get me wrong—anytime someone takes the time and effort to paint Jesus, I appreciate it." His humorous expression faded. "They definitely wouldn't be on my list of things to display, though."

"Someone appears to feel differently," I said. "The second theft involved an awful lot of effort to bypass a good alarm system."

"You don't think one of our clients had anything to do with this?"

I shook my head. "I doubt it. I volunteered here a few

years ago. You help good people. Outside your doors, however, there are plenty of unsavory individuals hanging around. A cop I know suggested it could be a Mexican gang."

"We don't have a lot of those." Father Abbott leaned back in his chair and steepled his fingers. "Not in the way you'd traditionally think of a gang, at least. No one's getting shot or stabbed over turf."

"I'm in the dark here." I spread my hands. "Any information you can give me will be helpful."

"There's definitely a criminal element," he said. "Every nationality probably experiences it. We help the people we can. Some are . . . beyond our reach. Others don't want our assistance. Instead, they take the easier route."

"You mean drugs."

"Probably. My understanding of more typical gangs is they have their hands in many pots. Drugs, extortion, prostitution . . . a litany of sins. The people who come here have a more singular focus."

"Do you know any of them?" I asked. "Could you point me to them?"

"I don't know their names," Father Abbott said.

"Would you tell me if you did?"

He nodded. "I wouldn't give up anyone who came in here. We're a sanctuary for all. Someone going against our work and harming our community, though? You're welcome to them. I wish I could help you more."

"Maybe you can," I said. "You seem to know a little bit about how these gangs operate. Remove the ugly factor. Why would they want paintings?"

"It's a good question." He leaned forward again. "I'm sorry I don't have a good answer to go with it."

"It's all right." We stood and bumped elbows.

"If you're interested in volunteering again," Father Abbott said, "we'd love to have you back. Do you speak the language?"

"Well enough to get by. I may look like a gringo, but I can hold my own."

"I suffer from the same problem." The reverend smiled.

"Does it make it hard for some of your potential clients to trust you?" I asked.

"Occasionally," he admitted. "Showing them I'm bilingual usually helps. Maybe it'll work for you, too."

If anything, I wanted to hide the fact I spoke and understood Spanish from the miscreants I was certain to encounter. Let them blab away while they think the handsome but clueless American PI doesn't know what they're saying. "I'd be willing to try just about anything," I said.

* * *

After some more fruitless sleuthing, I called it a day and drove home. Gloria greeted me with a kiss when I walked through the door. A fellow could get used to these sorts of things. We watched the local news, and then I adjourned to the kitchen to make something for dinner. A bag of tacos still dominated one of the shelves in my refrigerator. I opened a can of refried beans and cooked them on the stove while reheating the main course. It wouldn't count as my most innovative effort, but it would be very tasty with most thanks going to the cooks at Hacienda.

Gloria and I ate at my kitchen table and chatted about the day. She told me about enduring a long session of tennis practice. Gloria played the sport when I met her, and she continues to enjoy it to this day. She'd played in a bunch of tournaments in Maryland and the surrounding states. While she wouldn't take down Serena, I wasn't too proud to admit she would smoke me on the court. I've stood on the receiving end of her serves before and struggled to hit any over the net.

After we ate, I adjourned to the office on the first floor of my house. Despite renting a place, I maintained a laptop here for the times I didn't want to drive to Canton. As before, breaking into the city's surveillance camera system proved easy. I found the closest ones I could to Hacienda and accessed their feeds. Nothing jumped out at me. Traffic drove by at a normal clip. People walked up and down the surrounding streets. Workers occasionally popped out of the back door to smoke or throw trash away.

I left my viewer running while Gloria and I watched a movie. After it was over, I resumed my boring vigil. The clock struck ten. Hacienda would be closing. Car and foot traffic grew more sporadic as the hour hand advanced. About fifteen minutes later, a hooded figure walked down the street next to Hacienda. I leaned forward in my chair. The mystery man simply stood there. Following a brief interval, he dashed across the street and entered the alley behind the restaurant.

I could still see him, but the distance to the closest camera made it more of a challenge. As before, he simply stood there not doing anything. I didn't like it, however. Someone dressed much like this fellow broke into La Tolteca. At least then, he had the courtesy to do it after hours. At ten-twenty, a few late diners might still be inside to say nothing of the kitchen and wait staffs. I picked up my phone but put it back down. I didn't want to alarm Juan Manuel if it turned out to be nothing.

Hacienda wasn't a long drive especially at night. I grabbed my keys, climbed into the S4, and pulled onto Riverside Avenue at a speed not suggested by city planners.

* * *

As I APPROACHED HACIENDA, I called Juan Manuel. "Are you at the restaurant?"

"No, I left earlier." He paused, and dread filled his voice when he spoke again. "Why? What's going on?"

"It could be unrelated," I said, "but I used surveillance cameras to see what was going on. There's a guy with a hood in the alley behind your building. I'm almost there now."

"I'm on my way," he said and hung up. I turned off Eastern Avenue and left my car at the curb. The familiar heft of my Sig Sauer .45 at my side provided comfort when I padded across the street and into the alley. I hugged the building opposite the restaurant as I made my way down. The guy in the hoodie was gone, but he'd left his mark.

He spray-painted *Puta, les dijiste* on the back wall of Hacienda: Bitch, you told them. The black graffiti stood out against the beige siding. While it was bad, a larger problem revealed itself soon enough. Smoke billowed from a window near the rear entrance. People pounded on the door from the inside, and I noticed a bar shoved through the handle to prevent anyone from opening it.

I slipped a thin pair of gloves on during my sprint toward the door. The smoke thickened. I yanked the bar free, stepped to the side, and tested the handle. Not hot yet. I opened the door. A cloud of gray greeted me, along with a chorus of panicked voices. A few kitchen workers dashed out into the fresh air. I called 9-1-1 and then ran into the restaurant.

CHAPTER 5

I've run into a burning building before. After the first time, I determined it was an experience I never wished to repeat. About two years later, here I was doing it again. I shimmied past one cook making a beeline for the exit. Orange flames spread over the stoves and ovens all around me. The rear of the restaurant would be a total loss soon. I crashed through the swinging doors and emerged from the kitchen. A few people, most of them wait staff, screamed and beat on the front door. The arsonist must have rigged it in a similar way. "Back here! *¡Aquí atrás!*" I yelled in English and Spanish. Fire crackled behind me.

Finally, the deluge sprinkler system kicked in. Water doused the front of the restaurant. I hoped something similar happened in the rear. If not, Juan Manuel wouldn't be able to salvage much of this place. I herded everyone into the kitchen as they scampered through the swinging doors. "Avoid the right side," I said. "Stick to the left and go into the alley." Smoke stung my eyes, and a coughing spasm gripped me.

I staggered after the last person in the line and followed my own advice. The sprinklers worked back here as well, but water did little against most kitchen fires other than to spread the oil or grease. One of the waiters picked up a fire extinguisher and sprayed it all over the burning equipment. When the flames receded, he tossed it down and hurried for the exit. I shepherded him through, and we both coughed and stumbled into the fresh air of the alley.

Everyone stood a few feet from the wall, their eyes drawn to the black paint. I waved them farther along. "We need more separation if it collapses," I said. All seven of us moved about fifty more feet away. Between the built-in fire suppression systems and the waiter manning the extinguisher, Hacienda would probably stand to serve hungry diners another day.

Sirens rang out in the distance, getting closer. A car drove down the alley and screeched to a stop. Juan Manuel got out and checked on his employees. All of them said they were OK, and a couple pointed to me. When he approached, I directed the owner's attention to the back wall. "Shit," he muttered.

"This morning, a couple guys tried to discourage me from continuing the case," I said. "Apparently, everyone knows you talked to a PI."

"It's ridiculous." He stared at the black text. "I only told a few people."

"Then, one of them mentioned it to the wrong

people." The approaching sirens grew louder. "We can talk about it later."

Firefighters were first on the scene. They parked a truck in front and behind the restaurant, and a team dashed inside to assess conditions. Paramedics pulled up a moment later and checked on the workers who'd been trapped inside. I deferred until they were finished. My lungs no longer burned after a few minutes of breathing fresh air, and being out of the smoke did wonders for my eyes, too.

The cops arrived last. Between two plainclothes detectives and four uniformed officers, no one spoke a word of Spanish. Juan Manuel and I served as translators, with him doing a better job than I could. When the paramedics finished with the restaurant staff, they checked me out. Other than inhaling some smoke, I felt fine, and they soon gave me a clean bill of health. I hoped the same could be said for my clothes. The Orioles T-shirt I wore was among my favorites, but I needed it to not smell like soot after a trip through the washer.

The detectives waited for me as I finished. "Heard you were first at the scene," the older one said. He was tall, white, and slender. His partner was younger, black, and built like he bench pressed police motorcycles before breakfast. They showed me their badges—Friedman and Washington, respectively—and I returned the favor.

"You Rich's cousin?" Washington asked.

"Someone had to get the looks and brains in the family," I said.

"Tell us what happened."

I needed to be careful here. My knowledge of the

mysterious arsonist stemmed from my illegal access of the city's surveillance cameras. I couldn't come out and admit this to the police. "You might know a painting got stolen from another restaurant last night." Both detectives practiced their poker faces in response. "I drove here soon after closing time to see if anyone would try something similar tonight."

"You just happened to show up at the right time?" Friedman asked. Enough skepticism dripped from his voice to form a puddle on the concrete.

"Remember what I said about inheriting the brains in the family?"

"What did you see when you got here?" Washington said.

"Nothing, really," I said. "La Tolteca got robbed through the back door, so I walked into the alley. A guy in a dark hoodie ran away. I noticed the graffiti on the wall, and then smoke started coming out of the window."

"Sounds like you got here at the right time." Washington jotted a couple notes on a small spiral-bound pad. "Pretty lucky."

"You guys can be skeptical all you want. Yeah, I guess I got here at the right time, and it's a good goddamn thing I did. Otherwise, you're looking at six people dead, and the restaurant would be a total loss."

"Anything else?"

"Ask Captain Sharpe about me," I said. "Maybe the two of you can compare notes while you're deadlifting Buicks."

Washington grinned and closed his notebook. "We'll be in touch." He and Friedman walked away. Juan

Manuel was busy making sure his employees were all right and had a place to stay. I told him we would talk in the morning. He concurred. I drove home, still hoping I could get the smell of smoke out of my clothes.

* * *

Gloria doted on me when I returned. She was both concerned for my well-being and impressed with my bravery at the same time. I told her I'd run into a fire before, but the revelation didn't quell her worries. I took a shower, put on some fresh clothes, and then tossed my smoky ones into the washing machine. After guzzling a bottle of water, I plopped down on the couch beside Gloria as she watched the local news.

"All this for a missing painting?" she asked after a moment.

"Two of them," I said. "My guess is someone got pissed Juan Manuel brought me in."

"Who would know he did, though?"

"Good question. The pool should be small." I felt tired, but I wanted to look into this tonight. Juan Manuel didn't strike me as the kind of guy who blabbed his business to everyone. He didn't report the theft to the police and wouldn't have shared the fact he hired a private investigator with many people. Considering the late hour and what he had on his plate at the moment, I wouldn't involve him until the morning. I kissed Gloria on the cheek. "See you upstairs."

In my office, I looked into the people Juan Manuel was most likely to talk to: his family. His son owned the restaurant with him, but he made for an unlikely suspect. Even if he'd been involved in stealing the Garza, why would he torch his own business? Juan Manuel's wife only made occasional appearances at the restaurant. Their daughter lived in Virginia and had no involvement with the restaurant.

I came to Juan Manuel's grandson José Antonio. He'd recently turned twenty, and his record showed two juvenile arrests for assault. He was the right age to keep a bunch of social media accounts, and this made looking into him and his associates easier. Fifteen minutes into my search, I stumbled upon a TikTok video. José Antonio and another man performed a ridiculous drunken dance.

In the background, a Garza painting hung on the wall.

I paused the video, took a screen capture of the other man, and conducted a reverse image search. A Facebook profile popped up right away, and other similar accounts followed. Jorge Garza. I confirmed his lineage a few seconds later. His great-great-grandfather painted the picture on the wall in the video along with the two stolen so far in Baltimore. This made him a person of interest in my eyes. Considering the late hour, I opted against contacting him and instead walked upstairs to bed. Gloria was already asleep, so I settled in beside her.

In the morning, I opted against going for a run. The case demanded my time. I needed to talk to Juan Manuel and share my concerns. He'd probably defend his grandson, but he should know my suspicions either way. I put a pot of coffee on, scrambled some eggs, and dropped bread in the toaster. As usual, the morning kitchen aromas wafted upstairs and woke Gloria. She joined me a few minutes later.

Over breakfast, I told her about my late-night inquiry into the Espinoza family. "You think the grandson is capable of setting fire to the restaurant?" she asked after a bite of egg.

I sipped some coffee. "I don't know. It's a leap from assault as a teenager to arson as an adult. People have made it before, though. I want to talk to Juan Manuel first."

"Won't he stick up for his grandson?"

"Maybe. There's always a chance he doesn't like the kid. I don't think he would've talked to many people about what happened, though. Probably just his immediate family. José Antonio most likely heard it from his dad."

"I hope he doesn't cut off your access to tacos because you're accusing a member of his family," Gloria said with a grin.

"He's not a monster," I pointed out.

After breakfast, I uncovered José Antonio's phone number. People who are way too cavalier about their personal privacy leave it available on their Facebook profile. The youngest Espinoza could count himself among this dubious number. I eschewed my earlier plan to call Juan Manuel first and phoned the grandson instead. His voice sounded like I woke him from a deep sleep. It took a minute for me to establish who I was and for José Antonio to wake up. "Did you hear about the fire at your grandfather's restaurant last night?"

"He mentioned it right before I went to sleep." The

young man spoke English with no accent. He'd been born here. I wondered at his Spanish proficiency. "Sounds like it wasn't too bad."

"Some timely heroics prevented it from turning into a disaster." When he didn't follow the fact the heroics were mine, I filled in the conversational gap. "It could have been a lot worse."

"I'm glad it wasn't," he said, "but I don't know why you're calling me about it."

"You know anyone who would want to torch your grandfather's restaurant?"

"Why do you think I do?" A defensive edge dominated his tone.

"I don't think Juan Manuel told many people. What I don't know is how many additional people the first group told. Maybe you mentioned it to someone, and maybe he was involved in the theft of the painting."

José Antonio laughed, but I didn't hear a lot of humor in it. "You think someone's going to burn a place down over a painting? Have you seen one?"

"I have," I said.

"They're ugly. I know our families have been tight for a long time, but it's true. If you're going to light a building on fire, I think you'd want to put as many Garza paintings as you can in there first."

"You ever consider a career as an art critic?"

"I gotta go, man," he said before hanging up.

I didn't know what to make of José Antonio or our conversation. Ruling him out in any way would be impossible at the moment. All I knew for sure is I couldn't tell Juan Manuel what I suspected. He'd probably shut me down and maybe even give me the boot, which would leave him in the same predicament as before. It would also put a serious crimp in my future taco-eating plans.

In short, it was a lose-lose.

* * *

Gloria convinced me to stay a while. Once she kissed me and pulled my shirt off, the amount of persuasion needed plummeted to zero. As we lay in bed, our conversation drifted to my current case as it usually did. "It's so weird," she said.

"I still can't get my head around it all. The paintings are ugly. Their value is largely sentimental to Juan Manuel's family. Someone stole two of them, though, including one from another place. And then the mysterious arsonist tried to burn down Hacienda." I paused for a deep breath. "It's hard to see how any of this fits together."

Gloria's slow nod moved her chestnut hair just enough to make my nose itch. "Everything has to be related."

"You're right, I can't presume these are all disparate events," I said. "Stealing a painting and moving to arson is quite a leap, but someone made it. I need to assume it's the same person or people who swiped the Garza initially."

"You think the grandson is involved?"

"Maybe." I shrugged the shoulder Gloria didn't rest her head on. "I don't have a good reason to, really. It's why I haven't told Juan Manuel yet."

"Go make a case," Gloria said. She kissed me, rolled over, and stood. I got dressed, drank some more coffee in the kitchen, and left the house for my office in Canton Square. The drive from Federal Hill wasn't bad. Even though it added a couple minutes to my commute, I went by way of the city. The rowhouses of my home neighborhood yielded to the pavilions and tourist appeal of the Inner Harbor. Downtown Baltimore welcomed me with arms of glass and steel as I drove through. I picked up President Street, leaving downtown proper for its hotel-riddled cousin. A left on Fleet put me in Harbor East, but its upscale glitz soon turned into the blue-collar houses and pubs of Fells Point. I took Boston Street into Canton and my destination. In about fifteen minutes, the neighborhoods changed several times, and each could boast of being distinct in its own way. This drive was why I never took the highway to my office.

While heading down Boston Street, I noticed a vehicle behind me. I'd first spotted it on Fleet. Whoever was at the wheel made no effort to conceal the fact he was following me. Perhaps picking a generic-looking SUV and blending in with traffic emboldened him. I changed lanes, and my tail did the same. An amateur. Even a novice can carry a gun or call ahead to someone, however. As I sat idling at a traffic light, I kept a close eye on my rearview mirror.

CHAPTER 6

I TURNED OFF OF BOSTON STREET. THE CAREFIRST Building stood on my left, and the parking lot stretched out to my right. The SUV sped through the turn behind me. I swung a right into the lot and drove past several parked cars. Someone leaned out the passenger's side of the SUV holding a pistol. I made a sharp left as the first shot rang out.

My Audi S4 held advantages in speed and maneuverability. Being in a confined space gave back some of those, and the fact I didn't want to engage in a shootout near crowded buildings tipped the scales to my pursuers. I stopped the car, climbed out, and scampered behind the closest pickup I could find. The vehicle tailing me—which I could now identify as a Toyota RAV4—skidded to a stop behind my car.

I drew my .45. I didn't want to exchange gunfire in a public lot if I could help it. A few people walked to and from their cars. Our scene unfolded at the near end of the blacktop. Anyone using the far end may not see us past the other vehicles. Still, barking pistols would give us away before long. I got out ahead of things by calling the police. "I'm a private investigator. Two men followed me and have already shot at me once. Parking lot of the Care-First Building, Clinton Street." While the operator encouraged me to remain on the line, I broke the connection to concentrate on the men following me.

A quick peek showed the driver remained inside the RAV4. The passenger's door remained open. All the others were closed. It meant a single pursuer. I put my back to the front quarter panel of the pickup. Through the glass of a neighboring car, I spied a man skulking along the row. I inched my way down the truck. When I reached the rear fender, I leaned out with my gun at the ready.

The guy stalking me wore a mask. I didn't get to see much else before he dove for cover behind a BMW. Five parking spaces—three full and two empty—separated us. No vehicle sat across from the Bimmer. If he moved, I would notice. In a rare display of wisdom, the fellow stayed right where he was. If I leaned down far enough, I could spot his shoes near the German car's front tire.

Sirens broke the quiet. "What are you going to do, asshole?" I called. "You've already fired at me, so I'm more likely to shoot you than the cops are." The RAV4 drove down its row about a hundred feet. The gunman popped up, looked around, and dashed toward the SUV. I let him go. The door slammed, tries squealed, and the vehicle sped out of the lot.

A minute later, two police cars replaced it. I put my gun away and went to talk to the cops.

* * *

THE POLICE ASKED the usual questions. I felt a bit foolish for not noticing the RAV4's license plate. "In my defense, I was busy trying not to get shot," I said when Officers Jennings and Brennan stared me down like some rank amateur. "It's likely the car or the tags are stolen, anyway." They concurred, and the cops concluded their business a few minutes later when the forensics team drove off.

I rode the elevator up to my office and went inside. No masked gunmen waited for me. Getting past the dumpy security guard in the lobby wouldn't be much of an obstacle. I tossed my keys onto my desk and celebrated eluding a gunman by brewing another cup of coffee. Before I could even partake of a single glorious sip, Rich called. "I heard you got shot at," he said when I answered.

"I'm all right."

"You know who did it?"

"No idea," I said, "but my guess is it's connected to my case. Has the BPD reconsidered its stance on investigating art thefts?"

Rich snorted. "No."

"How about arson? Attempted murder?"

"Pretty big leap from stealing an ugly painting."

I sipped some coffee. Its taste remained untainted by my cousin's interruption. "I'm aware. I've done the same math . . . I simply did it faster."

"Whatever," Rich said. I pictured him rolling his eyes. He did it whenever I pointed out how much smarter

I was than the police, which happened regularly. "I just wanted to make sure you're all right."

"Thanks. I'm good." We hung up, and I considered my progress on the case. Other than running into a burning restaurant and getting shot at this morning, I hadn't done a lot. The closest thing I considered to a person of interest was my client's grandson. I presumed the arsonist and the two-man crew this morning were affiliated with whomever stole the paintings, but my deductions went no further than the obvious. The attention I'd attracted could prove problematic, however. I didn't need assholes with guns following me everywhere, especially when I wasn't working.

I called my semi-frequent associate Rollins. He's helped me out on several cases, and he rarely asked me to compensate him for his time and considerable expertise. As usual, he picked up right away. "What did you land in this time?"

"Art theft," I said.

He fell silent for a few seconds before coming back with, "Seriously?"

"I was a little surprised, too."

"Not sure how much I can help," Rollins said. "Just because I enjoy interior design doesn't mean I have much of an eye for art."

"Neither do the people who stole the paintings." I caught him up on all the details of the case, including the shooter in the parking lot.

"You want me to keep an eye on you?"

"It can't hurt," I said.

"Sure," Rollins said. "It might even help. I would've gotten the plate."

"Yeah, yeah. I'll give you a heads-up when I leave." I ended the call. With no other leads, I returned to the paintings. Everything started with them. I tried looking into the two missing ones but came up with nothing. A wider search turned up a result I didn't get before. A few days ago, the Mexican police seized a bunch of Garza paintings. The article was in Spanish, but I could follow it well enough. It didn't contain many details, however.

I remembered Paul King bringing up the drugs angle. Why would *los federales* seize a collection of hideous art? Even if they were as corrupt as movies and TV shows wanted us to believe, where was the money in taking paintings few people cared about? José Antonio Espinoza made a video with Jorge Garza. Did the descendant play some role in this mess? I tried calling José Antonio, but he didn't pick up.

Until now, I avoided telling Juan Manuel about whatever suspicion I harbored concerning his grandson. No time like the present to change course. I called my client but got his voicemail. I tried his home number next with the same result. For a man who always answered the phone, he was strangely unreachable, and I didn't like it. I called Hacienda next, but whoever answered told me Juan Manuel never came in, and the employee hadn't heard from the owner today.

I grabbed my keys and ran for the elevator.

* * *

Juan Manuel and his wife Sofia lived in the Charles Village area of Baltimore. His house on Guilford Avenue lay about fifteen minutes from mine. With the aid of fast driving, timely downshifts, and running a red light or two, I made it to his street in twelve. I parked in the closest spot I could find.

The houses here were of the row variety, too, but wider than most. Dormer windows jutted from the second floor. Columns supported awnings above the front porches. Parking was no better here, however—besides the street, most residents built pads in the back of their house. The sidewalk gave way directly to steps. Charles Village houses didn't get yards, either.

I darted up the stairs. The front door remained open a crack. "Shit," I said under my breath. I took a step forward and reconsidered. This didn't bode well for Juan Manuel and Sofia. However, whoever broke into the house could still be inside, and I was alone. I rectified the latter situation with a phone call. "Want to help me clear a house?" I asked Rich when he picked up.

"Do you think I don't have anything better to do?"

"Not really, no. I haven't been able to reach the restaurant owner all day, and he never went to work. I'm at his house. The door is open a crack."

"Could be bad," Rich said. "All right. Send me the address. Don't go inside without me."

"Sure thing." I texted Rich the location and leaned against my car while waiting. He sent a message telling me he'd arrive in five minutes. At the appointed time, his blue Camaro approached. He left it at the curb, and we walked to the porch together.

"You're lucky I was about to go to lunch." Rich looked at the entry and frowned. "The knob is scratched," he said, which I hadn't noticed. "Might not be anything, but it could be a sign of forced entry."

"We going in?" I drew my .45. Rich already held his 9MM.

"Let's do it," he said, his voice dropping to a whisper. Rich eased the door open, took a cautious step inside, and announced himself as the police. We entered the living room. Nothing looked amiss. We moved onto the dining room and kitchen, finding nothing unusual. Rich opened a door, checked it out, and said, "Powder room . . . clear."

I opened another door, leading with the muzzle of my pistol. Stairs went down to the cellar. There wasn't enough light to see anything else. "Basement," I whispered. "You want to go down?"

Rich shook his head. "Close the door. Let's go upstairs first." I did, and we took the carpeted steps to the upper level. Rich eased down the hall and cleared a bathroom. He peeked into the next room. "Bodies," he said.

"Shit." I walked in behind him. Juan Manuel and Sofia lay on the floor beside their bed. They'd both been shot in the back of the head. Dried blood collected around them. Rich crouched and felt Juan Manuel's neck.

"Not warm. Probably been a couple hours."

"Damn," I said. "First arson and now this."

"I'm going to check out the other bedrooms." Rich stood and left the room. He returned a moment later. "All clear. I'm going to call it in."

"We should check the basement."

"Why?"

"Maybe whoever shot Juan Manuel and Sofia came here looking for another Garza," I said.

Rich shrugged. "Could be motive, I guess."

"You see any paintings?"

He looked around. The walls were bare like they'd been in every room we entered. "I hadn't considered it before . . . but no."

"Then, they must be downstairs," I said.

"All right. We'll check it out after I call this in." We left the bedroom and started down the stairs. "Thirty Echo Alpha . . . I need backup and a forensic team to Twenty-Five-Ten Guilford Avenue. Two dead on scene. Plainclothes sergeant and private investigator in the house." An affirmative response crackled over the radio a few seconds later.

"I sometimes forget you're still a sergeant," I said as we approached the door to the basement.

"Never stopped being one," Rich said. "I just traded the basic blues for a suit a few years ago. I usually introduce myself as a detective because it's easier for people to understand. TV has taught them any officer out of uniform must be some sort of detective." He shrugged. "It doesn't come up very often."

"So you could pull rank on King?"

Rich grinned. "Might've done it a time or two."

I gripped the doorknob and glanced at Rich. He nodded. I yanked it open and stepped back. He started down the stairs gun first, and I followed. We descended into darkness, coming to a bare concrete floor. I flipped a wall switch on, and two overhead lights flooded the unfinished cellar. The hum of a nearby dehumidifier provided the soundtrack. Boxes and bins lined the walls, broken only by an occasional piece of old furniture. Toward the back, two wooden crates lay scattered on the floor.

The only thing left in them was a bunch of packing material. "Looks like whoever came here made off with some paintings," Rich said.

"And killed the homeowners. Still think this is just art theft?"

"Looks like you have a real case on your hands."

"Lucky me," I said.

CHAPTER 7

A SHORT WHILE LATER, THE MEDICAL EXAMINER rolled to the scene along with a trio of BPD crime scene technicians. Rich directed them to the various points of interest in the Espinoza house. We stood in the bedroom when the ME gave us the word. "I'd estimate time of death between nine and ten this morning," the slender man said. He pushed his wire-rimmed glasses farther up his nose. "Cause of death is the obvious. I can tell you more later."

"Thanks, Doc," Rich said.

"There's something else we need to consider," I said as I looked up Miguel Espinoza.

"What?"

"Juan Manuel's son was the co-owner. With Sofia dead, he's also next of kin. Not only do we need to notify him, we need to make sure no one's put a bullet in his head, too."

"He live far?" Rich asked.

"No." I showed him the map. "Few minutes."

Miguel lived on Brookfield Avenue in Reservoir Hill. Architecturally, the houses looked similar to those in Charles Village: brick and stone, wider than the average rowhouse but with rounded second and third-story fronts replacing the awnings. Rich and I went in his Camaro. I routinely mocked him for buying one with an automatic transmission, but my cousin possessed enough sense to get the V8. He knew how to drive it, too, and we made it to Miguel's house quickly.

I hoped we arrived on time.

The Camaro's tires kissed the curb in front of Miguel's house. We ran up the four steps and found the entrance closed and locked. A good sign. Rich used the knocker. A moment later, a Hispanic man of about forty opened the door. He frowned when Rich flashed his badge. "Detective Ferguson," Rich said, demoting himself for ease of understanding. "My associate is—"

"Also Detective Ferguson." I showed Miguel my credentials. "Your father hired me to look into the Garza stolen from the restaurant."

"Ah, yes." Miguel's eyes brightened. I dreaded giving him the bad news. "Come in, come in."

We walked into the living room and sat on the white leather couch. The carpet, recliners, and table supporting the TV were all the same color. It almost surprised me Miguel hadn't taken a can of spray paint to his flatscreen. "You live alone?" I asked when our host sat in the recliner closer to the sofa.

"For a couple years now," Miguel said. "My wife and I split up. She did all the decorating. I haven't bothered changing it."

"I'm afraid we have some bad news," Rich said.

"You can't find the painting?"

"Worse. I hate to be the one telling you this, but your parents were murdered in their house this morning. We just came from the scene. I'm very sorry for your loss."

Miguel sank back into the chair. His unfocused eyes stared straight ahead. After a minute, he closed them and took a few deep breaths. A tear ran down his right cheek. "What happened?" he said in a small voice.

"They were both shot," Rich told him. "We found them upstairs."

"In the basement," I added, "someone opened and emptied two wooden crates. Based on the packing materials, I'm going to guess they held more paintings."

"All this for some old shitty artwork?" Miguel rubbed his forehead. "I don't understand. My father always said the value of those things was all sentimental. No one would pay much for them. But last night, there was a fire at Hacienda. Today, you tell me my parents are dead. Killed."

I didn't know what to say. Rich may not have, either, but he'd done this a lot more than I had, so I deferred to his experience. "We're still looking into it," he said. "The police don't really get involved in art theft especially when the dollar value is low. The feds take over when the expensive stuff goes missing. We're coming into this fairly cold, but we'll figure out what happened."

Miguel's only reaction was to stare at the carpeted floor near our feet. Eventually, his eyes flicked to me. "What about you? You've been on this for a few days, now."

I didn't want to mention my suspicion of his son. Miguel didn't need another shock to his system right now. Besides, I didn't have a ton to go on yet. "I saw someone on a security camera near the restaurant last night." I felt Rich's glare on me but ignored it. "I don't know who he is yet. I'm still working on it."

"Work faster, dammit!" Miguel pounded his fist into his open palm. He looked away from us, and fresh tears ran down his face. "I'm sorry," he said after composing himself. "I guess I'm not handling this well."

"You're doing great," Rich said. "Do you have someplace to go?"

"Why would I leave?"

"You're the co-owner," I said. "Someone killed your parents, and we presume it was because of the paintings. You have a few stashed in your basement?" Miguel's deep frown served as an answer. "Whoever shot your mother and father is still out there, and yours could be the next name on his list."

"I'm not running and hiding." Miguel shook his head. "No way. Someone wants to find me, I'll be here."

His bravado was both predictable and foolish, but the conversation didn't need to go down this road. Rich offered protective custody, and Miguel declined. He said he would come in the evening to identify the bodies. With nothing else to ask and no succor to offer, we left. When we drove away, Rich said, "Now, what are you going to do?"

"Keep working this."

"When were you going to tell me about the man outside the restaurant?"

"When were you going to get involved in a case involving art theft?" Rich sighed. I couldn't even claim I told the cops who responded to the fire. I'd played it close to the vest even then.

Rich drummed his fingers on the wheel at a red light. "It's a double homicide. I'm involved, now . . . King and I both. Maybe you could do a little better at sharing information."

"I'll try," I said, knowing I would do nothing of the sort.

Rich dropped me off at Juan Manuel's house and kept going. While I drove away, I called Rollins. "Change of plans," I said when he picked up. "I'm going to wear my big boy pants. Someone else needs you a lot worse."

"Who?"

I gave him the rundown on what happened today. "Miguel won't accept protective custody, and he won't leave voluntarily."

"What would you like me to do?" Rollins said.

"Make him leave involuntarily."

"It can be arranged. I have a place in mind."

Of course he did. "Thanks," I said. "Keep him safe. The next bullet fired in this case might have his name on it."

"What if it has yours?"

For the second time this afternoon, I lacked a good answer.

* * *

A FEW HOURS LATER, I got a text from Rollins. *Got Miguel. He's safe.* When I asked how he'd managed to wrangle an unwilling man into some sort of protection, he offered only a simple response. *I'm very persuasive.*

I didn't doubt it. Back at my office—after confirming the grounds were free of people looking to shoot me—I conducted some more research into Juan Manuel's family. Nothing new jumped out at me. If José Antonio were involved, I couldn't find anything conclusive to point to him. He was my only suspect by default. I needed to do better.

As I did the previous night, I used the tried and true detective tactic of waiting for people to do stupid things. They rarely disappointed me. Tonight, I tapped into security cameras near La Tolteca. If whoever torched Hacienda and killed Juan Manuel and Sofia got what they wanted from his basement, it made sense they'd move on to their next target.

I watched on my tablet while sitting in my car parked a couple blocks away. About an hour into my vigil, the clock struck eleven, and a couple of miscreants appeared on the screen. I fired up the S4 and drove the remaining distance, parking on a side street. I skulked into the alley behind La Tolteca. Two masked men spray-painted the same curse word I found on the walls of Hacienda. Between them, a gas can sat on the concrete.

I snuck behind the one closer to me as he admired his handiwork. His friend spotted me at the last instant, but before he could shout a warning, I grabbed the vandal in a chokehold. He clutched my arm and fought for leverage. "Stop!" I shouted to the other one, but he scampered down the alley. The guy struggling with me elbowed me in the gut. I'd been too focused on the second criminal to stop him. To avoid it happening again, I seized my quarry's shoulder and spun him into the wall.

He rebounded off it quickly and led with a few punches. I deflected them all as I tried to get a look at this man in the flagging light of the alley. Despite the warm night, he wore a hoodie, and the mask obscured almost all of his face. Based on the little bits of skin I saw, my best guess put him as Hispanic. I blunted a couple of punches, stepped forward, and elbowed my attacker in the face. It rocked him back a step. I followed with a hard kick in his midsection. This folded him in half, and I dropped him to the alley with a knee to the face.

The guy was down for the count. I pondered what to do with him. I could call the police. This fellow and his partner probably set the fire at Hacienda and may have shot Juan Manuel and Sofia. If so, he'd be disinclined to talk to the police. He'd be working for someone, and if he lawyered up, the BPD would get nothing out of him. I couldn't call Rich because he'd follow the police manual chapter and verse. Paul King brought a certain moral flexibility my cousin didn't possess, but involving him still felt too official for now.

I took two zip ties from my pocket, bound the unconscious man's wrists and ankles, and left him in the alley while I fetched my car. A minute later, I threw him in the trunk and drove away. Once I left the immediate area of La Tolteca, I dialed Rollins.

CHAPTER 8

"You're burning up my line," Rollins said when he answered, which was on the first ring, as usual. "I might have to charge you double."

"You can have half my fee."

He chuckled. "Ain't it always the way? What's going on?"

"I found a couple assholes ready to light the second restaurant on fire," I said.

"Where are said assholes now?"

"One of them got away. The other is tied up in my trunk."

"You let one escape?" Rollins asked with a note of amusement.

"I knew I could only fit one easily," I said. "If I owned an SUV, I would have given chase. I want to talk to this asshole, but I need some place out of the way."

"I think I can find one. I'll text you an address in a couple minutes." He hung up, and I drove agonizingly close to the speed limit while I waited. The message came through in short order, and the address resolved to an auto repair center on Harford Road. I let the GPS plot the most efficient route and followed it. When I pulled into the parking lot, I saw Rollins' large pickup. The building looked rundown. Equal parts paint and graffiti covered its walls. It was structurally intact, though, which put it above several places we passed on the way.

Rollins climbed out of his truck. He was black and wore his hair very short, a holdover from his army days. While a little shorter than me, we probably weighed the same, and I figured he could outdo me in a bench press competition. He wore dark jeans and a black track jacket with a pink stripe framing the collar and running down the sleeves.

I backed into a spot close to the building and popped the trunk. The guy inside was awake, and he shouted a bunch of curses at me in Spanish. I punched him in the face, and this turned the lights out again. Rollins stood between my car and the street while I lifted the unconscious goon out and set him down at the rear of the car. "What is this place?"

"An auto shop my buddy owns," Rollins said. He unlocked the front door and entered a few numbers on the keypad. "Come on . . . bring the asshole inside." I jerked him to his feet beside me and held him upright while basically dragging him along. It would appear less suspicious to anyone who took note of us while passing by. Traffic was light at this hour, which helped our cause.

Once we were all inside, Rollins closed and locked the door. We carried the would-be arsonist into the repair bays. Rollins flipped the lights on while I set the man down in a chair. "What about Miguel?" I asked.

"He's good." Rollins hunted around on the shelves, rummaging through a bunch of tools.

"Anyone with him?"

"Yep."

"Someone you trust, I presume?" I said.

"Yep."

"You going to keep being monosyllabic?"

"Yep," he said.

The guy woke again, and once he shook the cobwebs off, he unleashed another string of curses. When he tried to get out of the chair, Rollins shoved him back into it and duct taped his arms down. The fellow made the mistake of attempting a kick, which earned him a punch to the jaw and a fresh strip of tape holding his legs in place. He kept yelling the whole time. Rollins moved back toward me.

"You speak Spanish?" I whispered.

"Not much. He saying anything important?"

"Depends how much stock you put into his opinion of your mother."

"Not much."

"He's also suggested we should both perform biologically impossible actions. I presume we're supposed to attempt them at the same time, but it's not clear."

"Creative," Rollins said. "You understand him?"

I nodded. "Most of it. I think he figures I don't, so I'm just letting him yell." After a fresh round of insults, the guy mentioned how his boss would find us and cut us into pieces. I whispered this to Rollins.

"Maybe we can find out who the boss is. Should be a few wrenches here somewhere."

"Hang on a minute," I said. "I'm not down for 'enhanced interrogation,' or whatever the current code word for torture is."

"I presume your love of the Geneva Conventions extends to me, too?" Rollins said. I bobbed my head once. "Fine." He walked to the bound man, who spat on him. Rollins stared at his track jacket, shook his head, and clobbered the guy in the chair so hard the whole thing fell over. He cursed us anew.

While Rollins wiped his clothes, I got our prisoner upright again. He insulted us the whole time. Finally, I interrupted him. "I speak Spanish, asshole. You're repeating yourself a lot. Didn't you learn any more insults?"

"Go to hell, gringo" he said, switching to English with a moderate accent.

"At least I'm in the company of Ambrose Bierce," I said. "Who's your boss?" He clammed up, and his eyes widened at my question. "Someone you're afraid of."

"*Sí.*"

"The guy you spat on shot an awful lot of people in the Middle East." I probably exaggerated Rollins' service record, but our prisoner in the chair wouldn't know. "He wanted to pull your teeth from your head one by one until you told us everything. I talked him out of it." I paused. "For now."

"*El jefe* will kill me."

"You're duct-taped to a chair, no one knows you're here, and my friend back there doesn't give a shit about your well-being. Why do you think you're better off with us?"

This forced him into silence. Sweat beaded on his forehead despite the fact it felt pleasant inside the building. When it became clear he wouldn't talk, Rollins held up a wrench. I provided a negative response. Maybe there was another way. I took out my phone and called up a picture of José Antonio. Our captive offered no reaction. I found a photo of Jorge Garza and showed it to him. His brows raised, and he swallowed hard. "This is *el jefe*, right?" I said.

"I don't know," he told me. "I work for him, but I don't know if he's in charge."

"In charge of what?" Rollins asked.

"Drugs. Between here and Florida."

"Why do you need ugly paintings?" I said.

The man shrugged as much as his restraints would allow. "For easy shipping."

There must have been more to this part of the story, but the fellow in the chair wasn't telling it. At least I knew the drug angle was right, and Jorge Garza held some kind of important role in the operation. I wondered anew if his friend José Antonio worked alongside him. With my phone still in my hand, I snapped a few photos of our guest and his many tattoos.

Rollins cut him free, and I bound his hands and feet with zip ties again. "You want out of Baltimore?" I said. "One-time offer. I'll drive you away from the city. If I see you back here again"—I jerked my head toward Rollins—"I won't talk him out of whatever ideas he has for you."

"*Sí.*"

We got in my car. I thanked Rollins for his time and drove up Harford Road toward Baltimore County.

* * *

WE DROVE through Baltimore County and into Harford County. I pulled into a parking lot, cut my prisoner's bonds, and encouraged him to leave. "Where will I go?" he asked when he climbed out.

"Anywhere you want. Delaware and Pennsylvania aren't far." He nodded and walked away without any further acknowledgement or thanks. I supposed gratitude would've been too much to ask considering Rollins and I tied him to a chair and threatened him until he spilled the beans. I turned around and cruised back home, pulling onto my parking pad well after midnight. When I walked upstairs, Gloria was already asleep. I quietly slipped in beside her and drifted off to dreamland in short order.

The next day after breakfast and a little more fruitless research, I drove into Little Italy. It was a few minutes before noon, and lunch patrons already walked into the many restaurants. I parked in the first open spot I could find and strolled through the door of *Il Buon Cibo*. A collection of carry-out orders waited at the front counter, and the seating area was sparsely populated. I looked for Tony Rizzo at his usual table, but he wasn't there.

Tony had been a friend of my parents for ages, and I'd known him most of my life. In addition to owning the restaurant, he also ran organized crime in Baltimore.

Years ago, I figured this out before my parents. They eventually put two and two together, and I imagined my mother's apoplexy at knowing a gangster to be epic. At Tony's spot, his daughter Gabriella sat with Bruno, the boss' right-hand man.

I walked toward them. Gabriella smiled and Bruno scowled, which were their usual reactions to seeing me. Tony's daughter was smart and beautiful, and over the last year or so, he softened his stance on her running things when he was gone. It constituted the best decision he'd made in a while. Despite my friendship with Gabriella, I knew there might come a day when we glowered at one another from opposite sides of a table.

Not today, however. We embraced, and she said, "It's good to see you, C.T., but my father isn't here today."

"I guess I'll settle for you, then." She grinned. Bruno, true to form, did not. "How is your dad?" I asked after we sat down.

"A lot better . . . thanks for asking. The warmer weather seems to have chased away his bronchitis."

"Good to hear." A waitress approached, but I shook my head.

"You're finally turning down a free meal," Bruno said. "I'll mark this day on the fucking calendar." He was middle-aged, tall enough to menace, and filled the chair at least as well as the goons who sometimes sat at the table. I'd dealt with him enough to know he didn't like me, and I didn't care.

"Good thing we're still in the middle of the month," I said. "I don't think you can count past twenty."

Bruno seethed, and Gabriella tried not to grin. "What brings you by?" she asked.

Normally, I would be careful to keep my voice low. Tony positioned his table several feet from any others, but with the dining room at reduced capacity, conversations became easier. "Drugs. Unless I miss my guess, your dad isn't very involved."

"You're right," she said. "He doesn't like them. As long as whoever sells them pays their share, he's happy to stay out of the whole mess."

"Anyone new coming to the tithing office?"

Gabriella shook her head, and her black hair shimmied. "No. Why?"

"I picked up a case," I said. "It started with someone stealing a couple ugly paintings. Turns out, the thefts are connected to drugs."

"You know who's involved?" Bruno said, reminding us he wasted his share of the nearby oxygen.

"I don't have names," I said, keeping my eyes on Gabriella. She was much easier to look at. "My suspicion is the packages are moving between here and Florida, and the missing artwork is involved somehow."

"I don't have any answers." She spread her hands. "Sorry."

Bruno cleared his throat. "You find out who these pricks are, I wanna know."

"You want me to give you updates," I said, "put me on the payroll. Consulting hours are noon to twelve-fifteen on the fifth Thursday of the month."

"Go to hell."

"Thanks for your time, Gabriella." I gave her a quick

smile, which she returned, and I stood. "Bruno. I would say it's always a pleasure, but my parents taught me not to lie."

Before he could spend the brain power on formulating a response, I left.

The fellow Rollins and I detailed told us how frightened he was of *el jefe*. He failed to provide us the identity of his boss, however, or even a clue as to who he or she might be. I didn't think it was José Antonio. He'd only been popped for a couple of assaults as a juvenile. He'd need to be a mastermind to pull off such an upgrade, and my conversations with the young man did not steer me in this direction.

Someone needed to be in charge. If not José Antonio, I figured he must've been involved somehow. It led me to wonder about Jorge Garza. He lived out of state. As far as I could tell, he'd never attracted the attention of police in Florida. He didn't even have a juvie record. Was he somehow a better candidate than José Antonio? I knew the guy we questioned worked for Jorge. It didn't make him the big boss, but it made him a player.

Like José Antonio, Jorge Garza recently turned twenty. He spent a year in community college and apparently decided it would be the crowning achievement of his academic career. Since leaving high school, Jorge Garza fought as an amateur boxer. Because every pugilist needs some sort of ridiculous nickname, Jorge's was "The Spider." As *noms des gants* went, it wasn't so bad. His favored trunks were red with a larger arachnid design twisting all over them. I even found a Spanish-language site which talked up the gains *La Araña* had made in the ring.

Next, I looked for information on drug arrests in Florida. This created a massive list. I would be ready to retire by the time I sifted through it all. Switching gears, I instead searched for drug seizures, which returned an even longer list. From here, I eliminated any case which led to an arrest. My workload went down about ninety percent. Jorge Garza spent most of his time in and around Miami, so I narrowed my geographic focus to the areas he frequented.

I was left with a manageable number. Each record held a few photos and contained notes of varying quality and completeness. After skimming through a couple and feeling my eyes glaze over, I searched for names of interest and studied the pictures. About eight records in, I saw the one I needed. A brick of cocaine sat on an unadorned table. Law enforcement seized no other drugs or weapons. It was a small victory as these things went, but they touted it just the same. The accompanying report mentioned no name I cared about.

The photo mattered. The white powder was wrapped in a clear bag dominated by a red spider design and sealed with black tape.

CHAPTER 9

José Antonio Espinoza and Jorge Garza were friends. Ample evidence supported this. I could also make a convincing case for Jorge being a drug trafficker. Were the two men in business together? I couldn't connect those dots yet, so I set about doing it. Jorge would need a connection in Baltimore, and who better than the descendant of his grandfather's compatriot?

My first step needed to be establishing a pattern of drugs in transit from Florida to Baltimore. Driving them remained a possibility. Interstate 95 earned a nickname as "the Iron Pipeline" because of the illegal guns traversing it on a regular basis. Jorge was young. He was a card-carrying member of the instant gratification generation. Sending cocaine by car would take about fourteen hours of continuous driving and expose the operation to plenty of outside problems.

Flying remained the best choice. The time involved would be much less. A small plane taking off from a tiny airport and landing at another would be subject to far less scrutiny than a vehicle on the open road. Bribe a couple underpaid employees, pay a pilot, and you established a reliable way to move product a thousand or so miles in a couple hours.

I hunted for minor airports. They only needed a runway and a tower. If a Cessna could take off and land, it would be enough. I knew of several such places around Baltimore but had no idea of their Florida counterparts. More research turned up a few which saw frequent drug raids. I eliminated those—Jorge was young but not stupid.

Each facility maintained a website. They didn't accommodate things like reserving a flight time, but they'd be on the same network as the rest of the systems. I accessed the database of the first with a simple injection attack. The defenses against these have been well-known for years. They've also been poorly implemented, which made my job easier. The flight manifests contained no records of travel to or from any place near Baltimore.

I kept digging. The second and third airstrips were also swings and misses, but I found something at the fourth. Their website proved harder to break into, which meant the company could be hiding more important data. Their database didn't succumb. However, an outdated WordPress plugin gave me a way in, and I took it. From there, I found a couple of credentials and used one to access the required information.

Three times in the last two months, a small plane took off from Hurricane Airfield—which struck me as an unfortunate name—and landed at College Park Airport. Flight manifests showed a pilot, no crew, and two boxes of art as the cargo. A different person manned the cockpit each time. Jorge tried for some obfuscation, booking the trips under Araña Art Restoration LLC. The business listed a Florida registered agent as the point of contact, but there was enough here to establish Garza's involvement.

Now, I needed to make the case to the BPD.

* * *

"You want to do *WHAT?*"

Captain Leon Sharpe of the Baltimore Police Department fixed me with his well-practiced stare. It was a pretty good one. Sharpe was tall and large, built like a defensive end who spent his spare time bench pressing motorcycles. I figured he shaved his bald black head with a katana. Over the last three or so years, I'd been on the receiving end of his glare enough to no longer be intimidated. It would be quite effective on new officers, though.

"I want to go to Miami and bust an interstate drug operation," I said.

"So go." Sharpe shrugged. "You seem to have all the facts." He gestured toward the copious data I printed and provided him.

"I'm not exactly licensed to operate in Florida."

"Neither are we," Sharpe said.

"Probably a lot easier for you to overcome the bureaucracy."

The captain leaned back in his chair. Despite his rank, Sharpe sat in a pretty small office. He was an old-school cop—the kind who favored kicking in a door, cracking a few skulls, and hauling someone off to jail. It didn't fit in with the kinder, gentler image the BPD tried to cultivate. He got results, however, and suspects being found and arrested makes everyone look good. "Let me guess . . . you want to take Rich with you."

"King, too," I said. "Call us a task force. It's not like I've never worked with the department like this before."

Sharpe frowned and leafed through the pile of papers I presented him. His traditional tendencies extended to the way he preferred to ingest data. After a moment of review, he said, "So this Garza asshole is a boxer who calls himself The Spider?"

"*La Araña*, technically, but yes. They all need a nickname."

"And the art on his trunks has turned up on some bricks of coke."

I nodded. "A pared-down version also appears on small bags sold in Florida and Baltimore."

"It's not exactly an airtight connection." Sharpe took off his reading glasses and set them atop the printouts. "I might be able to get a warrant with it, but I'd want to take it to a friendly judge to be sure."

"We can keep building the case from Florida," I said.

"Can we? Wow. Thanks, I've never run an investigation before."

"Always happy to help, Leon."

Sharpe rolled his eyes, but the corners of his mouth struggled not to turn up in a grin. "I'm sure we can make some arrangements with our colleagues to the south." He picked up his desk phone and mashed three buttons on the keypad. "You and King come to my office," he said a few seconds later.

A couple minutes later, Rich walked into Sharpe's office followed by Paul King. The latter saw me and said, "Oh, fuck. What are we doing now?"

"Pursuing justice and glory," I said, "in equal measure . . . and in a really nice location."

Sharpe's office held only two guest chairs. Three other people in its confines definitely made a crowd. Rich snagged the other seat, forcing King to stand. The captain slapped the pile of papers on his desk and caught everyone up to speed on what I'd discovered. "We know anyone in or around Miami?" Rich asked.

"We'll make it work," Sharpe said. "The commissioner can grease the wheel for us."

King sat on the corner of the desk. "All right. We're in."

Sharpe stared at King until he moved. "All right. I'll get started on the paperwork. All of you pack your bags. I want you in Florida as soon as possible."

I DROVE HOME and threw a few days' worth of clothes in a suitcase. Toward the end, I added a bathing suit. Investigations took time, and I could spend some of it at the beach. "I wish I could come with you," Gloria said as I zipped my bag.

"Me, too," I said, "but we'd never fit all your luggage on a small plane."

She smiled. "You're probably right." I was. I could pack a single suitcase to last several days. Gloria took the bags-to-days ratio and inverted it. Any time we traveled, it looked like we were moving into the hotel. She sashayed to me and eyed my bag on the bed. "How soon do you need to leave?"

"The BPD is still working on all the arrangements. We probably have some time."

Gloria grabbed my shirt and pulled me into a kiss. "Let's not waste it, then."

We didn't.

About an hour later, Rich texted me the flight information. I threw my clothes back on, grabbed my luggage, and bade Gloria farewell. "Be careful," she said. "Drug traffickers sound pretty serious."

"The guy in charge calls himself the spider." I shrugged and gave her my most confident grin. "I've swatted two this week. How bad could they be?"

A few minutes later, I set off for Martin State Airport. It sat in Baltimore County in the town of Middle River. While much smaller than BWI, it still served the area with a good number of flights. Its single runway saw a lot of traffic. We tried for College Park to inspect the operation, but they claimed no availability. I pulled into a parking lot next to Rich's blue Camaro. Our plane, a small two-engine puddle jumper, waited in a hangar. "Didn't know the BPD sprang for a private flight," I said when I joined my cousin and Paul King.

"We're trying to make sure people down there don't get word of what's going on," Rich said.

"Don't worry," King added, "we're flying coach on the way back."

"*You're* flying coach," I said. "I'll upgrade my ticket."

A few hours later, we checked in to our hotel. I let

Rich and King go first, and I overhead the clerk telling them they'd be sharing a room. When they were finished, I paid to change to a king-bed suite. Later, we walked a few blocks to the beach and setup our towels on the sand. The stifling heat of midday was behind us, but even as the dinner hour neared, it remained plenty warm. Because I burn at the suggestion of sunlight, I applied plenty of sunscreen.

After Rich and King enjoyed a brief dip in the Atlantic, we all sat on our towels. I watched a trio of women walk along the sand. Their bikinis struggled to hold their breasts in and stay together at the same time, and I wondered if each woman's next step would be the one to end the fight. "We need to get our operation up and running tomorrow," Rich said. "I'm going to reach out to the locals tonight."

"Can we work from here?" I asked.

"We'll probably be in the city limits."

"No, I mean right here . . . on the beach." The ladies walked past. Their bathing suits kept up the fight. Judging by the reactions of some fellow beachgoers, I wasn't the only one disappointed in the outcome.

Rich smirked, but his eyes followed the trio of buxom beauties. "What would Gloria say?"

"Probably something similar to Jeanne."

"Fair enough."

"You two think about your girlfriends," King said. "I'll keep an eye on the local ladies. You never know who might be carrying a concealed weapon."

We left a short while later when the sun began its descent in the western sky. After a quick shower and change of clothes, I ate dinner with Rich and King in the hotel bar. Rich said a local cop would stop by later to review jurisdictional matters and the like. I got the feeling my presence wouldn't be required, and I didn't mind. It sounded boring, and I tried to remove myself from the system whenever possible.

Later, Rich told me we enjoyed latitude to conduct an investigation but needed to bring the locals in for arrests. "Let's start at the airport in the morning," he said.

"Sounds good. I have a couple ideas."

He sighed into the phone. "Will I like any of them?"

"Probably not," I said.

CHAPTER 10

THE THREE OF US SAT IN A PARKING LOT AT Hurricane Airfield. Our rental car was a white Chevy Impala, and despite its light color, the midmorning heat and lack of shade required us to run the air conditioner. Since we'd been here, two flights took off, and another one landed. King took pictures of the employees he saw. I sipped mediocre coffee and opened the facility's website on my tablet.

I skipped the photos, testimonials, history, and other puff pieces. The *Our Staff* page would at least tell us something. Sure enough, it listed names, photos, and brief biographies of key personnel. Whoever wrote them graduated from the University of Boring. The information provided, however, made it much easier for me to search for data on these people.

Frank Wright, the lead mechanic, lived a nondescript life. I couldn't find evidence of a parking ticket let alone involvement with drug runners. He went onto the unlikely pile. The three tower employees lived similarly clean lives. In their case, it stemmed from the fact they needed to pass federal background checks to hold and keep their jobs. The government's investigators would find nothing juicy in their pasts.

"What are you doing?" Rich asked as I brought up the page for facility manager Henry Thompson III. In his picture, he looked like he played football in high school and then spent the next twenty-five years telling people about it when he wasn't eating. If we needed to chase him, I liked our odds.

"A little research," I said as I read his bio.

"The legal kind?"

"Why do you put such onerous requirements on me?"

Rich sighed and shook his head, but his next question betrayed his underlying practicality. "Find anything?" On the surface, he loved to play things by the book, and it sometimes created tension between us. At the end of the day, he wanted to put criminals in jail. Sometimes, I found the best way to do it, and Rich would go along with it. After a bit of moralizing, of course.

"Not yet," I said. "I'm looking into the manager now." I began my research by connecting remotely to my computer, which the BPD believed was part of its network. From there, I could access state police resources, which allowed me to tie into other locations. Like Florida. Henry Thompson III, in addition to his job as the manager of Hurricane Airfield, also owned a single-person LLC.

"Did you change rooms?" Rich said.

"Yes."

"Why?"

"A double bed?" I scoffed. "I'm neither fourteen nor traveling on the company dime."

"Is the king bed to your liking, your majesty?" Rich said.

"It's all right," I said. "Someone on hand to fluff the pillows would be nice."

Rich rolled his eyes, but he and King both snickered. Engines roared behind us as another plane built up speed and took off. Thompson's other enterprise, Freight Movers Consulting, purported to help small businesses find the best way to ship small and large packages across the country. I wondered if this extended to bricks of cocaine originating from south of the border. The LLC's extremely basic website remained silent on the issue.

Thompson owned a small house about fifteen minutes away. He drove a seven-year-old Hyundai. On the surface, he wasn't living beyond his means. Next, I looked into the company's financials. Despite the business address resolving to a UPS store, the LLC owned another property. I did a double-take when I saw it. Five bedrooms, four bathrooms, a pool, and a three-car garage. Thompson couldn't afford it on five times his salary, yet real estate records indicated Freight Movers Consulting paid cash for it a year ago.

This was before Jorge Garza began moving drugs as far as I knew. Thompson clearly provided his "consulting" services for others in the drug trade. Whoever owned Hurricane Airfield either didn't conduct a thorough investigation into their employee or enjoyed a percentage of the take. "Got anything?" King asked.

“The manager’s dirty,” I said. “He makes seventy a year, and his LLC paid cash for a million-dollar house in a nice neighborhood.”

King spread his hands. “I’m sure he’ll tell us he’s lived a frugal life.”

“He’ll be full of shit, then.”

“Why don’t we go ask this asshole some questions?” Rich said. He got out of the car. King and I followed suit.

We walked into the main building. It was long and squat and may have been a trailer in a past life. Much of the walls on either side of the door were replaced by glass, lending the place a very open feel. It didn’t contribute a lot of natural light this early, but it would later in the day.

For his part, Thompson filled out the area behind the counter pretty well. He wore a white button-down, and his belly hung over his dark blue jeans. A blue tie--not the same color as his pants--stopped somewhere above his navel. Thompson stood, though a desk with a heavy-duty office chair sat a step or two away. He eyed us suspiciously as we came in. I silently blamed Rich for giving off cop vibes. King looked like a failed rock singer, and I was way too good-looking to be pegged for police. "Help you?" he asked while scrutinizing us--Rich in particular.

"We're looking for a flight," King said.

"Where to?"

"Baltimore."

"Miami airport ain't far," he said.

"Too many people." King shrugged. "I don't like to attract a lot of attention."

Thompson pointed at Rich. "Why do you travel with him, then? He looks like a cop."

"He's my security detail." King said.

"What about him?" Thompson jabbed his finger toward me.

"I'm the token handsome member of the group." I said.

Thompson's frown told me our explanations didn't mollify him. "Can't help you. I'm booked solid right now."

I made a show of looking around the place. A tiny waiting area consisting of a coffee table and two ugly plastic chairs sat unused. A cobweb hanging between two legs adorned one of the chairs. "Sure . . . looks like you're really beating them off with a stick here."

My comment earned me a stare. I didn't quake or tremble. "Like I said, I can't help you."

"Too bad," King said. He took his badge out of his pocket and tapped it on the countertop. "I was hoping you'd be able to assist us."

"Got nothing to say to the cops. I run a clean operation."

"The hell you do," Rich said. He flashed his shield, too. "You don't want to talk to us? Fine. We'll call the feds, and they'll take this place apart."

Thompson put his hands on the counter. "I ain't scared of them. Ain't scared of you, either."

"Were you afraid of your English teacher?" I said. I reached into my pocket and closed my hand around a lock-blade knife.

"Screw you." He pointed at Rich and King. "I saw your badges. Why would I give a shit about a couple Baltimore cops?"

I pulled out the knife and flicked it open with my right thumb. With my left hand, I yanked Thompson's tie. The knot tightened around his neck, and his body bent toward us. I drove the knife into the tie, pinning it to the counter. Rich glared at me. King smirked. "Look, asshole. We're not really here for you. We're looking for one of the people who make frequent drug trips out of your shitty little airfield."

"Don't know . . . anything," Thompson said. The knot at his throat made his face redden. He reached for the knife but couldn't remove my hand from the hilt. The sharp edge pointed toward him, so he couldn't use it to rip the fabric and escape.

"Too bad," I said. "You'll probably pass out soon. When you hit the ground, this place will probably fall down around you."

"Or you could help us," King said. "Tell us what we need to know, and we're gone."

"All right . . . all right."

I rocked the knife back and forth, which made withdrawing the blade easier. Thompson straightened and sucked in a deep breath. "What the hell?"

"Answer our questions," Rich said, "and you won't have to see us again." Thompson shot me another glare--I again felt very non-intimidated--and nodded. "We're looking for someone who's done a few flights from here to Maryland. We think he landed at College Park Airport."

Like me, he probably felt salty we couldn't depart from there.

"What was he flying?"

"Drugs. I don't know what the manifest would say, though."

"Probably art," I added.

"Name?"

"Jorge Garza," Rich said.

Thompson entered the name on a keyboard. Recognition flashed in his eyes as he looked at his monitor. "OK . . . yeah. He's flown out of here before. Always to the airport you mentioned."

"He scheduled to again?" King asked.

"Yeah." Thompson nodded.

"When?"

"Tonight."

Rich said," What time?"

"Flight leaves at nine-thirty." Thompson said.

"When does he get here?"

"No TSA checkpoints here." He shrugged. "Usually a half-hour early. Not much cargo to load."

"How many people?" Rich asked.

"Usually five," Thompson said. "Garza, his pilot, and three guys who look like they played for the Dolphins."

"Lot of security," I said.

"Tough business. We don't provide a lot of protection. The other place probably doesn't, either."

"All right," Rich said. "We're going to come back tonight. We probably won't be alone. You tip off Garza in any way, and I'll have the feds so far up your ass, they'll know what you ate for dinner. We clear?"

"Crystal," the harried manager said.

"Good. See you tonight." We left. When we were back in the car, Rich kept talking. "I'm going to bring in the locals to make the arrests. Hopefully, we'll wrap everything up quickly."

"I don't trust this guy," King said. "We need to be ready for shit to go sideways."

"We will be," Rich said.

CHAPTER 11

THE THREE OF US MET AN EQUAL NUMBER OF LOCAL cops at Hurricane Airfield. Outside the main building, Corporal Ortiz greeted us first. He was a tall, burly Hispanic man, and bumping elbows with him felt like slamming my arm into a brick wall. He introduced us to Deputies Brown and Wilson, a white man and woman, respectively. Brown's head of wispy white hair sat atop a wiry body. Wilson looked to be about my age, and short blonde hair framed her serious face. "Thanks for catching us up," Ortiz said after the round of introductions. No one in the Florida party seemed to care I was a private investigator.

"Sure," Rich said. "I presume you've all seen Jorge Garza's picture?" They nodded. "He and his party should be here soon. Getting on a plane isn't illegal, so we're going to wait for him to load his cargo. Once he does, we'll inspect it. You brought a dog?"

Ortiz nodded. "We did. They're waiting out of sight near the hangar."

"Good. Let's make our way over." The six of us walked down the narrow road. The former trailer shielded us from view. After about a quarter-mile, we got inside the hangar via an unadorned steel door. The building itself looked like a small warehouse. A large garage door allowed aircraft to come and go. In the center of the concrete floor, a plane waited. It was an old enough model to have two propellers rather than jet engines. A forklift and a bunch of other equipment lined the walls.

A couple minutes later, the phone rang. Ortiz picked it up, said, "Thanks," and set it back on the hook. "Garza and his party are headed our way. It's him, a pilot, and three bruisers."

"Just like we figured," I said.

We all took up positions behind the forklift and other equipment. Two SUVs pulled up outside. Their engines died, and a minute later, two goons walked in. After them, the pilot entered, followed by Garza. The third enforcer brought up the rear. No one in the group appeared happy to be here. For a man who figured to make a lot of money soon, Garza looked despondent. Maybe perverting his ancestor's art weighed on him.

After everyone made a circuit of the plane, two of the hired musclemen went back outside. They dragged crates on wheels when they returned. The two of them lifted each into the cargo hold while everyone else got on board. Once they finished, another local deputy led a German shepherd into the hangar. The six of us stepped out from hiding.

"Jorge Garza and party," Ortiz said. "We have a warrant to search this plane and anything on it." The aircraft's door remained closed. Ortiz shoved the paper at one of the goons. He scowled at it, and I wasn't sure he could read it. "Open the cargo compartment."

"Piss off, pig," one of the enforcers said.

Ortiz punched him in the stomach, doubling him over. After a second of sucking wind, the large man sank to all fours. "You open it, then," Ortiz said to the other one.

"I like him," I whispered to Rich.

He rolled his eyes in profile. "You would."

The second guy opened the hold. Ortiz and Brown dragged one of the crates out. Brown contributed little to the effort, and even the goon smirked at Ortiz doing most of the work. Brown used a crowbar to pry the top off. It took him a while, but he kept at it. Ortiz didn't rush him or take over, maybe because he did almost all the heavy lifting a moment ago.

Wilson took a parcel out. Brown paper enveloped it, but it was the right size to be one of the stolen Garza paintings. The dog trotted to her, sniffed the item, and offered no reaction. Everyone in the Florida contingent frowned. "Can we get back to work now?" the goon asked. His partner regained his feet and let out a couple of weak coughs.

"Not so fast," Ortiz said. He took a knife from his pocket and sliced open the paper. It held a Garza framed by wood. The art itself was set in the front of the frame, leaving at least an inch and a half behind it. Nondescript brown bags were stuffed into the empty space. He held one of these out to the dog, but the pooch again remained quiet. "This is bullshit." Ortiz cut the bag and set it atop a small table.

It was plastic wrapped tightly around several bags and enveloped in brown waxed paper. Some of the bags held coffee. Others held potpourri. Several contained a white powder, and these featured the large red spider design Garza fancied. Ortiz held one out to the dog, who barked immediately. "What do we have here?" he asked the pair of enforcers.

The one who didn't get slugged in the gut raised his hands. "I only signed up to guard some art shipments."

"Really? You're going to stick with such a lame story?"

"It's a competitive business," he said.

Brown and Wilson cuffed the two goons, with Rich and King providing support in case either rebelled against their smaller adversaries. Ortiz hollered toward the plane. "Jorge Garza! No surprise we found drugs in your cargo. Come out with your hands up. Same for your pilot."

The door didn't open. Instead, the propellers fired up. Everyone who had ever seen *Raiders of the Lost Ark* backed away. With Rich and King keeping eyes on the goons, the Florida crew drew their pistols. Never one to be left out, I did the same. Ortiz shouted again, but I couldn't hear him from a few feet away. The plane lurched forward and turned toward the right. We all followed it. "Hold your fire," Ortiz said. "We don't want to hit the fuel tank and turn this place into an inferno."

I wanted to educate him on how gasoline worked, but a drug trafficker trying to escape made this a poor time and place. Once it neared the wall, the plane swung hard to the left. It kept going in the new direction until it spun a one-eighty. The pilot steered it away from the large door and toward the entrance we used. Everyone moved well clear of the props as the aircraft stayed as close the wall as it could—knocking a few tools over in the process —and headed toward the far end of the hangar.

As it neared the wall, the pilot cut it hard to the left. On the other side of the fuselage, the stairway dropped and scraped along the concrete floor. Garza hired a skilled operator—he stopped right at the door. Someone dashed down the steps and left the building as the props wound down. The way the aircraft sat, the stairway blocked our exit completely.

"I'm calling the DEA," Ortiz said. "This is a major bust with or without Garza."

"We can't let him get away," I said.

"We've crippled his operation."

I shook my head. "Rich, you want to catch a fleeing asshole?"

"Sign me up," my cousin said.

"You guys don't have arrest authority!" Ortiz shouted as we headed toward the other end to take the long way around.

"Too bad the guy who does is more interested in calling the feds," I said.

He scowled. "Wilson, go with them."

She ran after us.

* * *

Only one SUV sat outside the hangar. When he bolted clear, Garza climbed in one and sped away. We didn't see him anywhere as Rich drove the rented Impala from Hurricane Airfield. I sat up front, and Wilson took the back seat. "Where the hell are we going?" my cousin asked.

"I'm working on it," I said, already reviewing information on Garza via my phone.

Wilson's mobile was pressed to her face. She turned away from us to talk as quietly as possible. Rich shot her a glance in the rearview mirror. "The DEA is coming," she said after a moment. "They're sending a team to take the two hired hands into custody and confiscate the drugs."

"And shut you out of the rest of the investigation," I added.

She frowned at me. "I'm not in this for the glory."

"You're probably also not in it to watch someone else steal your work and hog all the credit." I shrugged. "You do you, though."

Wilson rolled her eyes. "We know where this asshole would go?"

"I have a couple of possibilities," I said. I used my phone to connect to my main PC in Baltimore via an encrypted tunnel. The console required a lot of typing, a process not aided by Rich driving over every pothole in Florida. "His girlfriend lives pretty far away. If he's trying to get somewhere quickly, he wouldn't go there. His LLC points to a registered agent. Probably some nitwit we could intimidate another address out of."

"Could take too long," Rich said. "Some people are

really good at hiding where they're really working from. Keep looking."

"Who put you in charge?" Wilson said.

"I'm a sergeant. How about you?"

"A sergeant in *Baltimore*."

"A major in the Marines still outranks a captain in the Army," Rich said.

Wilson sighed and seethed. I kept looking for any place Garza might use to hide out until the heat died down. A new result popped out at me, and I spent a moment looking into it. "Garza boxes, and he always trains at a certain gym."

Rich glanced at me. "So?"

"Guess whose LLC just bought it," I said.

"How are you looking all this up?" Wilson said. She sat forward as much as the seatbelt would allow.

I canted my phone screen away from her prying eyes. "I moonlight in real estate."

She snorted. "The hell you do."

I held my left hand under my chin. "You don't think this face could sell a nice house?"

"What's the gym's address?" Rich said. I keyed it into the car's GPS. It showed us we were seven minutes away. Rich mashed the accelerator. We'd probably make it in five.

* * *

The Impala didn't move with the urgency of Rich's Camaro, but it did pretty well. We got to the gym in five minutes thanks to some aggressive driving. Rich circled the place. It sat on a corner. No lights were on in the front. When we drove past the side of it, though, some illumination showed from the back half.

And a man with a gun on his hip walked a perimeter.

Rich circled back to the main road and curbed the car across the street. "You should stay here," Wilson said to me. "You're a civilian without a gun."

"I can't fix the first part," I said, "thank goodness. I can get a gun, though."

"What do you mean?"

"Wait here." I pulled the handle and got out of the car.

"We'll be behind you," Rich said.

Wilson threw up her hands. "Is this how you do things in Baltimore?"

I smiled. "This is nothing." I closed the door slowly and quietly. While Rich and Wilson got out and squabbled at a whisper, I dashed across the street and parked myself at the corner of the building. No sign of the sentry. I padded down the side and stopped just before reaching the back wall. I peered around and saw the man on duty turning around and heading my way. Rich and Wilson crept close behind me.

"He's coming," I said in a quiet tone. Both cops held their guns in their hands.

When I heard his footsteps approaching, I stepped out from hiding. The guard did a double take but didn't make a move for his sidearm. I took out my phone, faked looking at it, and slipped it back into my pocket. "Has this always been a gym?" I asked.

The guy shrugged. "Is now. We're closed."

"You box?" He shook his head. I walloped him in the stomach, elbowed him twice in the face, then dropped him to the asphalt with a hard kick. "You might ask your boss for a lesson or two."

"I don't think he can hear you," Rich said as he and Wilson joined me. I relieved the unconscious sentry of his pistol and phone, spiking the latter onto the lot and breaking it. He fell near a rack mounted at the rear of the building. Rich took out a zip tie and bound the man's wrist to one of the metal posts.

I checked out his semiautomatic. It was a classic Colt 1911 .45. I checked the magazine and found it full but the chamber empty and racked one in before thumbing its safety on.. "Ready to go in?" I said.

"I'll take the front," Wilson said. "You two go in here. Give me a couple minutes before you breach."

"Roger," Rich acknowledged. We walked to the rear entrance as Wilson trotted around the building. He tried the knob. "Unlocked."

"Are we really going to wait for her?" I asked.

"Teamwork. I let you run off and get a pistol. We're not going to be cowboys now. We'll let Wilson get in position, and then we'll go in."

Considering Rich stood closer to the door, and I couldn't open it around him, I was forced to go along with his plan. To pass the time, I pondered the resistance we could meet inside. "He can't have many men. Garza's not a big trafficker yet. The three goons and a pilot are probably most of his payroll."

"Let's be ready, anyway," Rich said. "Even assholes

have friends . . . especially when they have money or drugs to spread around."

"We'll see." I glanced at the watch on my wrist. "She must be in position by now."

Rich nodded but didn't make a move. "We'll give her a few more seconds." After the appointed time, he eased the door open and padded inside. I followed him and stopped right away, catching the door and easing it shut. Darkness greeted us. We moved slowly down the hallway while our eyes adjusted. Rich and I cleared each room in the corridor. All were empty.

As we approached the center of the building, the light increased. A boxing ring dominated the floor. Someone set up a few chairs around it. On the other side of the squared circle, a few punching bags awaited their abuse. Free weights lined the right-hand wall, and jumpropes hung on hooks. No one moved around the area. We also didn't see any sign of Wilson. She should've made her way into this part of the gym by now. I voiced my concern to Rich.

"Maybe she's taking her time up front," he whispered. "Let's keep going." An office and another door awaited us on the other side of the ring. The smaller room was for storage, and while messy, it was free of evildoers. The office remained. We approached the door. Something shuffled behind us. I turned around to see Jorge Garza and one of his goons pointing guns at us. How did they hide from us?

"Drop your guns," Garza said.

CHAPTER 12

Where was Wilson? She should have been here by now. Rich and I held onto our pistols. Raising them would be a death sentence. Jorge Garza and his hired gunman would shoot us both dead, and we'd be lucky to squeeze off a single round in return. I deferred to Rich on how to play this scenario. My cousin sized up our adversaries, so I did the same.

"I said drop the guns," Garza repeated.

"Where the hell were you?" I said.

He showed a cockeyed grin. "We hid under the ring when we heard you open the back door."

"We didn't come here alone," Rich said. "You'd be wise to surrender now."

"Why do I need to surrender?" Garza asked. He spread his left hand wide. The right still held a gun pointed at us. "I'm a man who owns a boxing gym. You two broke in here and started poking around. I can shoot you, and no one would bat an eye."

"You'd be gator food," the goon added.

"He's right," I said as a sidebar to Rich. "I think he could toss us into a wood chipper and still claim self-defense in Florida."

"Listen to him." Garza inclined his head toward me. "Put down your guns, and maybe we can all walk away."

"You'll be walking away in handcuffs," Rich said.

"For owning a gym?"

"For smuggling drugs."

"You think a kingpin would own a place like this?" Garza said.

"Maybe," I said. "If he needed to steal his ancestor's paintings, then he might."

Garza narrowed his eyes at me. "The artwork belongs in my family. It shouldn't be displayed in a restaurant."

"*Señor* Garza was a religious man. How do you think he'd feel about a brick of cocaine stuffed behind his paintings of Jesus?"

At the end of my question, I heard a soft click come from the front of the gym. Garza and his goon showed no sign of noticing. I kept my eyes forward. In my peripheral vision, Wilson walked up the stairs and into the main part of the gym. She navigated her way past the weight benches and heavy bags without making a sound. Rich gave no indication he saw her, but I knew he did. We both turned slightly, and Garza and his man mirrored the movement. Wilson could approach from directly behind them now.

I hoped Wilson reached us before the staredown ended in a shootout. Rich and I both had guns leveled at us, and ours pointed toward the shabby floor. While Wilson's approach was quiet, she also kept it slow to avoid tipping off Garza and his goon. My pulse pounded in my ears. I contemplated what moves I could make if the whole situation went to shit in a hurry. None of them were good.

Wilson made it to within fifteen feet. This was a large gym, and most of the main area around the ring remained open and navigable. The enforcer's eyes flicked to Garza. He remained focused on Rich and me. So far, neither of them noticed the woman. She proved very good at sneaking. We just needed her to close the final few paces quickly.

"This is your last chance to surrender," Rich said.

"No," Garza said, "it's yours." His eyes flashed a murderous glare.

My finger applied a bit of pressure to the trigger. I prepared myself to drop into a rapid crouch while squeezing the trigger as quickly as possible. I didn't know what Rich planned—his clear edge in experience probably led him to devise something better—but similar thoughts must've turned over in his head.

Before I could ponder the ramifications of an extrajudicial gunfight, Wilson pressed the end of her pistol into the back of Garza's neck. When the goon saw what happened, I rushed forward and inserted myself between him and Wilson. I grabbed for his gun. He didn't want to let it go. I kicked him in the side of the knee. His leg buckled, his grip loosened, and I pried the firearm away from him. Then, I hit him in the head with it, dropping him to the dingy wooden floor.

I pivoted. Wilson tried to restrain Garza, but he shook her off. Rich barred his arm as he tried to raise the gun. In the struggle, both their weapons clattered off the parquet. Garza threw a solid right cross, showing his boxing training. Rich blocked it. After each man turned away a few more blows, Rich hit him with a short jab in the stomach, then a strong hook to the face. The blow forced Garza to spin toward Wilson, who dropped him with an elbow just below the eye. So much for *La Araña.*

"What took you so long?" I asked Wilson as she cuffed Garza. Rich picked up the would-be drug mogul's fallen gun and dropped it into an evidence bag.

"The front door was locked," she said. "It took me a couple minutes to pick it in the poor lighting. I also radioed for backup before I came in."

Rich handed her the bag and grabbed one of Garza's arms. "Probably a good thing you got here when you did."

"Nonsense," I said. "We had things well in hand."

Rich rolled his eyes. He shoved Garza toward the back of the building. Wilson crouched over the fallen goon. I joined her. "He'll be fine. He's barely bleeding." I slapped him hard. His face screwed up in pain, and his eyes fluttered open. "See? Rise and shine, asshole. You've got an appointment with a small cell."

Wilson and I—mostly me—hauled the man to his feet. She zip-tied his wrists together and we led him toward the back of the gym. On the way, Wilson radioed Ortiz, and we learned he was only a couple minutes away. Rich and I exchanged fist bumps.

* * *

Ortiz arrived a few minutes later with a handful of uniformed cops in tow. They herded Garza and his goon into two police cars and drove away. "We'll get to keep them until the feds come calling," Ortiz said.

"The state of Maryland might want a piece, too," I said. "They could bring arson and murder charges."

"Way above my pay grade." Ortiz shrugged. "These two are fucked for a long time. I don't really care about the rest."

"What about the paintings?"

"Evidence."

"Some of them are missing from Maryland," I said. "It would be nice to take them home."

"Take it up with the feds," Ortiz said. "They'll probably want to hang onto everything."

I'd hoped to get the stolen artwork back for Miguel Espinoza and Ricardo. With the DEA taking over, it looked like a swing and a miss. We all piled into a few cars and headed back to their precinct. En route, Rich called Sharpe. Thanks to the captain's booming voice, I heard both sides of the conversation. "Captain, we picked up Garza."

"Good work," Sharpe said. "I have a few people surveilling Jose Antonio. We'll grab him, too."

"Sounds good," Rich said.

"You coming back tomorrow?"

"Should be."

"Good," Sharpe said. "I'll expect the usual level of

detail in your report." He hung up. Rich looked slightly less displeased than normal.

Arriving at the precinct, I was disappointed to see it looked a lot like Rich's in Baltimore. BPD South in Florida featured more windows but lacked much of a view. In the daylight, it may have looked better. Wilson assumed the position at the coffee station. No one stopped her, so I objected. "We wouldn't have made the bust without her," I said, nodding toward Wilson. "Someone else can work the machine."

Ortiz frowned. "She's new."

"Must be nice to have the woman make the coffee. Where's the wood paneling and shag carpet?"

"For Christ's sake." Ortiz stomped to the brewing machine and picked up where Wilson left off. He muttered while the magic liquid dripped into the pot. I chose to ignore him. It's a rule of mine in a police station to only drink java I've personally witnessed being brewed on my current visit. How the cops drank the sludge which sat around for hours would always be a mystery to me.

Once we were all armed with fresh steaming cups, we gathered in Ortiz's office. He dialed Leon Sharpe and put the call on speaker. After a moment for introductions, Ortiz said, "We wrapped everything up tonight. Garza is in custody, we seized a bunch of his drugs, and we arrested three enforcers, plus a pilot."

"I'm sure the Baltimore contingent acquitted themselves well," Sharpe said. He didn't mention Rich's update.

"Some of us especially so," I pointed out.

"A few of us stuck it out and did the hard work, Captain," King said. "We couldn't all sit on the beach and do a lot of typing."

"Too bad. We might have broken the case sooner."

"I'm glad to hear everyone contributed," Sharpe said. "Rich, King . . . you'll need to file reports when you get back." I leaned back with my arms behind my head and kicked my feet up onto the corner of Ortiz's desk. He shook his head and fought a laugh.

"I might spend a few days at the beach," King said. "I'm sure my sergeant can handle the paperwork for me."

We hung up with Sharpe a moment later. "Thanks for coming down here," Ortiz said. "All of you. We haven't run a lot of joint operations with Baltimore before. This is something to build on."

We all shook hands. Rich, King, and I left the building and climbed into our Impala. "I'll set up our flights for tomorrow," Rich said once we were underway back to the hotel.

"You might want to make them in the afternoon," I said. "It sounds like your partner is desperate for some fun in the sun."

King chuckled and pointed at me. "I ain't the only one who enjoyed the beach."

"I'll see what I can do," Rich said.

"Will you be joining us on the plane, sire?" King asked.

I smiled. "Once I upgrade my ticket, sure."

"You're seriously going to fly first class?" my cousin said.

"Rich, please. How long have you known me?"

"Way too long."

I let the predictable barb pass. "My philosophy on flying coach is the same as sleeping in a double bed."

"At least you're consistent," King said.

Either man could have offered further uncharitable comments. Neither did. I took the win.

* * *

Back in my hotel room, I sat on the bed and called Gloria. We exchanged pleasantries and I-miss-yous for a moment before she got to business. "How's the case going?"

"Wrapped it up tonight. Everyone's in custody, and whatever operation Garza had running is dead."

"Awesome," she said. "Are you coming home?"

"We're heading back tomorrow." I kicked my shoes off and stretched out. How could a grown man sleep in a double bed? "Rich is making the arrangements."

"You're flying coach?" I envisioned Gloria wrinkling her nose. We didn't always see eye-to-eye on the finer things in life—she was even more fanatical about some things than me—but we were in lockstep when it came to planes and hotels: go first class or go home.

"I was disappointed Rich thought I would," I said. "I'm heartbroken you'd think so little of me."

She chuckled. "Just make sure he doesn't lock you into some ticket you can't upgrade. It would be like Rich to try something like that."

"It would, but I'll be wise to his tricks."

"Tell me how the case went down." Gloria always

wanted to know the details. She worried about me, and when I told her in person, she frowned, clutched the table, or clenched her hands into fists. I figured she'd be reacting similarly as I relayed the tale of researching Garza, going to the airport, his attempted getaway, and the showdown in the boxing gym. "It sounds like a good thing Wilson got there when she did."

"Probably," I said. "Rich and I might've found a way out of it, but I think we were both happy to resolve it without any gunshots."

"How was the beach?" Gloria asked, changing gears.

I paused a beat before answering, and I knew it would give me away. "Who said anything about going to the beach?"

"You're in South Florida, and I know you. How was it?"

"Incomplete without you," I said.

"Good answer," Gloria said.

CHAPTER 13

THE NEXT DAY, I MADE USE OF THE HOTEL GYM before breakfast. It was a hot, soupy morning outside, and I didn't care for running outdoors in those conditions back at home. Here, I could make use of a treadmill, so I did. It's never the same as pounding the pavement, but I finished my four miles in about thirty-six minutes before returning to my room for a much-needed shower.

Rich and King had almost finished breakfast when I joined them. They stayed and enjoyed an extra cup of coffee each. I grabbed a bowl of oatmeal, a yogurt, and the last hardboiled egg from the breakfast spread. We made light conversation as I ate my food and drank two cups of coffee, snagging the second only moments before the hotel workers took the spread down.

Ninety minutes later, we were back on the beach. We didn't have long to stay, so I joined my cousin and King for a quick swim in the ocean. The heat and humidity couldn't keep the attractive beachgoers away. As before, we watched several women with interest. I liked King's theory about concealed weapons, and sharpening the old observational skills always proved a good use of my time.

After a quick shower back at the hotel, we piled into the Impala for the drive back to the airport. After breezing through security, I made a beeline for the airline desk and changed my seat from coach to first class. It doubled the cost of the ticket, but I was only paying the difference, so I didn't care. The extra legroom alone would be worth it, to say nothing of the superior food and drink options. I stretched out, enjoyed a beer shortly after takeoff, and ate a sandwich once we were at cruising altitude. To rub it in, I snapped pictures of both and sent them to Rich and King. They probably wouldn't see them until we landed—the Wi-Fi in coach was an add-on, and neither man was likely to pay for it.

When we landed at Martin State Airport, my phone buzzed. I checked my messages. Rich sent me a selfie with him and King flipping me off. We chatted a bit as we left the terminal for the parking lot. I said I'd try to stop by and go to lunch with them tomorrow, and they insisted I pay because I could afford to upgrade my hotel and flight. With no counterargument, I simply nodded and got into my car.

Rather than drive home right away, I stopped by Hacienda. The restaurant was still closed, and a sign on the front door promised a quick return in Spanish and English. A light came from inside, so I knocked. A couple minutes later, Miguel appeared. He waved me inside and locked the door again behind me. "What happened in Florida?" he asked when we both sat at the bar.

"We got Garza and the people in his operation."

"My father is avenged."

"I'm sorry for your loss," I said.

Miguel nodded. "Thank you. I'm glad you caught the bastard. What about the paintings?"

"The feds have them, I'm afraid. Moving drugs across state lines brings them in. Because Garza used the artwork to smuggle his drugs, they're all evidence. I honestly don't know when you'll get them back."

He snorted. "Or if."

"Or if."

No mention of Jose Antonio. I didn't want to ruin the mood by telling him. Miguel reached across the bar and picked up two shot glasses and a bottle of bourbon. He poured us a couple fingers each. He raised his glass. "To my father."

I did the same. "To your father." We drank our bourbon, and then I left.

* * *

THE NEXT DAY after a morning run and breakfast with Gloria, I got the call I'd been expecting. "Hi, Mom."

"Coningsby, is this story in the paper accurate? You and Richard went to Florida and stopped a drug ring?"

"I haven't read it, but the major detail is correct." My parents still received The *Baltimore Sun* on their porch—or their lawn, driveway, or wherever the carrier tossed it—every morning. They seemed to think I read it, too. If I bothered reading a newspaper, I'd do it digitally. Every now and then I read the articles of my own exploits. They made good fodder for my website and Facebook page.

When one operates a *pro bono* detective service, one is glad to receive free publicity.

"That must have been exciting."

"It was." I left out the salacious details of the beach and the unsettling details of the encounter in the gym. My mother was a worrier by nature, and I didn't need to add any fuel to the fire. "We closed down the whole operation. Another person will probably emerge to fill the gap soon, but he'll be someone else's problem."

"You're very cynical recently, Coningsby." Her tone mirrored the one she scolded me with as a teen. I heard it often. "Are you all right? Are things going well with Gloria?"

"We're fine, Mom."

"I'd be happy to go ring shopping with you one day, dear."

"Mom!" I looked around to see if Gloria lurked nearby. The coast was clear. "It's not in my plans right now."

"Very well." She returned to the topic at hand after a delicate sniff. "It's a shame the man who hired you died."

"His son is very glad the case is closed," I said. I didn't mention his grandson's complicity. It might have made the paper, anyway.

"I'm sure he is," my mother said. "You should come by for dinner soon. We always love seeing you and Gloria."

I considered offering to bring a bag of Hacienda's finest tacos but decided against it. My mother wouldn't eat something for dinner unless she could put it on a nice plate and cut it with a knife and fork. "Sure. Let's do it one night this week."

"Very well, dear. Your father and I will wire the usual amount into your account later today."

"Thanks, Mom."

"Goodbye, dear."

We hung up. Gloria popped back into the room. "Getting paid by the parents soon?"

"Yep."

She dropped onto my lap and put her arms around my neck. "Where you taking me?"

I leaned in and kissed her. This went on for a moment before I wrapped my arms around her waist and lifted her from the couch. She let out a squeal of delight. "How about upstairs?"

"I like the way you think," Gloria said.

While we ascended to the second floor, my phone rang. I ignored it. A new case could wait for a new day.

THE END

THANKS FOR READING! C.T. Ferguson will return with a new novel soon. Each book in the series stands alone. You can start with C.T.'s first case in *The Reluctant Detective*.

AFTERWORD

Hi! Thanks for reading this novella. I hope you enjoyed reading it as much as I did writing it.

Here are the other books in my catalog:

The C.T. Ferguson Crime Novels:

1. The Reluctant Detective
2. The Unknown Devil
3. The Workers of Iniquity
4. Already Guilty
5. Daughters and Sons
6. A March from Innocence
7. Inside Cut
8. The Next Girl
9. In the Blood
10. Right as Rain
11. Dead Cat Bounce
12. Don't Say Her Name

13. Night Comes Down

The C.T. Ferguson Crime Novellas:

1. The Confessional (book 1.5 in overall series continuity)
2. Land of the Brave (2.5)
3. Red City Blues (3.5)
4. Blood on Canvas (8.5)

The John Tyler Action Thrillers

1. The Mechanic
2. White Lines
3. Lost Highway
4. Four on the Floor
5. Forced Induction (early 2023)

I release 3-4 new novels per year. For the most updated catalog, you can visit www.tomfowlerwrites.com or https://books2read.com/tomfowler.

While these are the suggested reading sequences, each novel is a standalone mystery or thriller, and the books can be enjoyed in whatever order you happen upon them.

Do you like free books? You can get the prequel novella to the C.T. Ferguson mystery series for free. *Hong Kong Dangerous* is unavailable for sale and is exclusive to my readers. Visit https://www.subscribepage.com/hkd2020 to get your book!

Connect with me:

For the many ways of finding and reaching me online, please visit https://tomfowlerwrites.com/contact. I'm always happy to talk to readers.

This is a work of fiction. Characters and places are either fictitious or used in a fictitious manner.

"Self-publishing" is something of a misnomer. This book would not have been possible without the contributions of many people.

- The great cover design team at 100 Covers.
- My editor extraordinaire, Chase Nottingham.
- My wonderful advance reader team, the Fell Street Irregulars.

www.ingramcontent.com/pod-product-compliance
Ingram Content Group UK Ltd.
Pitfield, Milton Keynes, MK11 3LW, UK
UKHW021648190726
13853UKWH00001B/126

9 798201 767761